Wrong Train to PARIS

Wrong Train to PARIS

Romance on the Orient Express

JENNIFER MOORE

Covenant Communications, Inc.

Cover: *Woman* © Ildiko Neer / Trevillion Images; *Cherry Blossom Photo* by Mark Tegethoff on Unsplash; *Eiffel Tower Photo* by Jungxon Park on Unsplash.

Cover design by Michelle Fryer
Cover design copyright © 2020 by Covenant Communications, Inc.

Published by Covenant Communications, Inc.
American Fork, Utah

Printed in the United States of America
First Printing: December 2020

27 26 25 24 23 22 21 20   10 9 8 7 6 5 4 3 2 1

ISBN 978-1-52441-438-2

PRAISE FOR JENNIFER MOORE

"This leisurely, rose-colored romance from Moore (*Solving Sophronia*) makes for delightfully soothing reading . . . All this sweet story requires is for readers to sit back and allow it to gently whisk them away."

—*Publishers Weekly*

"Delightful and charming! Readers' hearts will go out to Julia as all her attempts to be useful backfire and she finds herself more and more deeply indebted to Luc. A sweetly delicious story full of the landscape and flavors of Provence. A new favorite."

—Julie Daines, author *It Started in Budapest*

"In *Wrong Train to Paris* by Jennifer Moore, readers will lose themselves in the romantic French countryside as Julia Weston grapples with thwarted plans in taking the wrong train, putting her at the mercy of rural farmer Luc Paquet and his quirky aunt Gabrielle. Julia tries to make the best of her predicament until the next train comes, yet everything seems to go wrong. Readers will root for both Julia and Luc as they navigate through one sticky situation after another in this delightful romance full of charm, wit, and sigh-worthy scenes."

—Heather B. Moore, author *Until Vienna* (coming April 2021)

"Endearing characters throughout. Jenny's setting details are just as fascinating as her love story. I was rooting for Julia on every page."

—Jen Geigle Johnson, author *Song of Salzburg* (coming August 2021)

FOR DAVE LUNT AND JEFF DOTTL
Provence will always remind me of you.

AND FOR RICHARD KIMBALL,
whose creativity fills the world with remarkable art

ACKNOWLEDGMENTS

I WILL EVER BE GRATEFUL to those who make it possible for me to spend my day in a fantasy world. My family supports me when I head out of town on a writing retreat. They have microwave pizza and cereal for dinner when I'm working through a deadline, and they understand when I'm late to pick up for carpool because I got caught up in my story.

The first person who comes to mind when I think of Provence is my brother Dr. Dave Lunt, who lived there and made me fall in love with a place I've never been. Merci, mon frère.

Thank you, Chris Miller, for helping me with my French.

Thank you to Michelle Lucas for answering all my goat-related questions.

Thank you, Tori Gordon, for telling me all about your chickens, their laying habits, and their colorful eggs.

Thank you, Clarissa Wilstead, for teaching me about grafting olive trees.

Thanks to Nancy Allen, Josi Kilpack, Ronda Hinrichsen, and Becki Clayson for helping me plot this story.

Most of all, thank you to Julie Daines, Heather Moore, and Jen Johnson for coming up with this series idea and letting me be part of it. I have loved working with you talented women.

CHAPTER ONE

Spring 1900

THE TRAIN PLUNGED INTO DARKNESS, lit only by the weak light of the gas lamps, dimmed for daytime. The car went quiet as the travelers shifted uncomfortably in the strange gloom. Julia Weston paused in the act of setting a stack of playing cards on the table. She looked toward the window, seeing only the reflection of the interior of the lounge car against the black of the tunnel and her own face staring back at her.

The faces of her companions were reflected in the glass as well: one stern middle-aged woman, one distinguished older gentleman, and one—she noticed her gaze rested too long on Herr Klausman and pulled it away lest he see her staring—one handsome younger man. A blush crept over her cheeks.

She let her gaze move over the train car's other occupants and attempted to appear as if she were not looking at one spot in particular. The noise of dishes and conversation had quieted, almost as if the tunnel had cast some sort of spell over the passengers. Julia was always amused by the way people stopped whatever they were doing and stared out the windows when there was nothing to see. Perhaps it was simply human instinct for one's attention to be drawn to the unexpected.

Though aspects of the journey, such as a game of cards with a handsome gentleman, were far from ordinary, the trip itself was exceedingly familiar.

Julia had made the journey between Vienna and Paris often enough over the years, but this was the first time her father—busy with preparations for the World's Exhibition—had been unable to accompany her. And since Colonel Weston, retired from the British army, would not hear of his daughter traveling alone, he'd found a companion to accompany her.

And Frau Maven snored at night.

Splendidly.

Julia stifled a yawn. She did not believe she'd slept one minute in the compartment adjoining the older woman's the night before, but it was too late to take a nap now, and if she fell asleep after dinner, she'd miss her stop at Igney-Avricourt. And that wouldn't do at all.

She kept her gaze moving, thinking if she allowed it to rest in the dim light, she might fall asleep. Her eyes met Herr Klausman's again, and she jolted, fully awake.

Julia had always considered the train very romantic. And perhaps this time—without her protective father's accompaniment—it would be romantic for *her*. She loved this train. The elegance of the furnishings and the passengers were a sight one did not get used to. Travelers hailing from all over the world journeyed on the Orient Express, and the variety of languages and costumes surrounding her filled her mind with imaginings.

She kept her focus on the darkness, wondering if Herr Klausman was watching her reflection. The idea was rather pleasant. The man possessed many qualities she valued. He was handsome, of course, and his clothing and manners were impeccable. He sat straight-backed in his chair, his fair hair was parted precisely, and he was punctual, a habit Julia considered among the most important in a person's behavior. He had come into the lounge car for the card game seven minutes earlier than their arranged time—eight minutes after Julia herself had arrived.

She blinked as the train emerged and sun shone again through the windows.

Frau Maven cleared her throat and motioned toward the cards in Julia's hand.

Julia set them down and straightened the stack carefully, sliding the smaller piles to her three companions. She took the last for herself, then turned over the top card, placing it next to the center stack.

Herr Klausman, seated across from her, lifted his cards and spread them into a tidy fan, moving a card here and there into order. "And I hear zeh grand tower has been painted a ghastly yellow," he said, his German accent thick. He raised a brow and curled his lip in a complicated expression that indicated his disapproval of either the color or, more likely, Monsieur Eiffel's creation itself. It somewhat ruined the effect of his handsome face.

But the gentleman was not alone in his opinion. Many—especially among the artistic community of which Julia was particularly associated—still considered the Paris monument a disgrace—an atrocity of mangled steel towering over the skyline of the most beautiful city in the world, a colossal

waste of money and resources. Others admired the contemporary structure
as a marvel of modern architecture comparable with America's Washington
Monument. Strong feelings existed on both sides of the argument, and it
was still hotly debated by all Parisians, from wealthy financiers, heiresses,
and clerks to street performers and penniless urchins.

As for herself, Julia adored the tower, having watched its construction
as a child and viewed it with nostalgia each time she returned to Paris.

"A most extraordinary creation," the man who had introduced himself
only as Nicholas, sitting at Julia's right, replied with a nod. "Even still, eleven
years after its creation, she is zeh tallest structure in zeh world. She has zeh
strength of iron, yet zeh lines are so graceful. Elegant." He hooked his curved
pipe back beneath his thick black mustache, then swept his hands wide, lifting them to a narrow point in imitation of the tower's shape. "A true masterpiece." He spoke the words slowly, drawing out the last and infusing it with
a dramatic flourish.

Julia arranged her cards both by suit and in numerical order and then
spread them evenly in her hand.

"A masterpiece indeed." Frau Maven nodded and smiled sweetly.

Julia's companion, a stern-faced widow from Austria, had agreed with every
statement either of the men had made so far, making the conversation, in
Julia's opinion, rather dull. The older woman sat to Julia's left with her back
to the train's window, wearing fresh lip rouge and a colorful silk scarf with her
beige traveling clothes. Neither accoutrement had been present when Julia
and the older woman had boarded the train late the previous evening at the
Vienna station, nor had they appeared at any time over the nearly fourteen-
hour journey until just an hour earlier, when she'd entered the lounge car. Not
only had Frau Maven's attire been drab and free from color of any kind, her
temperament had seemed to follow the same course. Julia had not heard a kind
word or seen a hint of a smile on the woman's face until the two gentlemen
had introduced themselves, joining them for luncheon in the train's dining car
earlier that day. The transformation that came over the older woman had been
astonishing, to say the least. She'd not only smiled and spoken quite cordially
but had actually giggled—often.

When the men had proposed an afternoon card game to pass the dull
hours before dinner, Frau Maven had practically fallen over herself to accept.

After a moment of deliberation, Julia played a card, and Nicholas set
one atop it almost immediately.

"A *gut* choice, sir." Frau Maven beamed across the table.

Nicholas smiled. He didn't appear to have even given his cards more than a quick glance, but he'd managed to win nearly every hand—even when his partner, Frau Maven, was so distracted. He was dressed in black from the top of his hat to the toe of his shoe, and his hair and mustache followed the color scheme exactly. His look was unique and distinctive, with an old-style pipe in his mouth, although in the hours they'd spent together, he'd yet to light it. He apparently considered it a distinguished-looking ornament rather than a functional item.

Julia couldn't be certain of the man's age and estimated him to be near to fifty years old, but she would not have been surprised had his true age deviated fifteen or more years in either direction. His accent she could not place. He spoke English, French, and German easily, as did the others, moving between the languages throughout the course of their conversations, but in every language, his accent remained—not quite identifiable.

Adding to the peculiarity of her new acquaintance, Julia thought Nicholas looked familiar, though she couldn't say from where she might have known him. Perhaps their paths had crossed at one time in an art museum. Or maybe they had taken the same train before. Try as she might, she couldn't place him.

An attendant approached, and Nicholas scooted his chair forward, giving the man more room to pass between himself and the stools bolted beneath the bar behind him. Nicholas and Herr Klausman had pulled the table away from its place beneath the window and set a chair on each side. The arrangement was much more conducive to a card game but less convenient to those walking past along the narrow aisle.

After a moment of deliberation, Herr Klausman lay down a card. "Und at zeh Grand Exposition, you will also see the world's largest wheel. Taller than one hundred meters, if you can believe it."

"Oh my." Frau Maven touched her breastbone.

At last we are speaking of something interesting. Julia had anticipated riding in the Grande Roue since it was announced months earlier. "Yes," she said. "When I left Paris in January, it was nearly fin—"

"You will be quite overcome by zeh structure's size, I believe, Miss Weston." Herr Klausman continued as if he'd not heard her reply. Or, apparently, anything else she'd said, as this was not the first time in the past hours she'd mentioned she'd lived the majority of her life in Paris. He did seem rather less handsome the longer she was acquainted with the man.

"Of course, it is much too frightening for a gentle young lady to ride inside such a dreadful creation." Herr Klausman shook his head. "You would do well to avoid it."

Julia narrowed her eyes. Why did people constantly underestimate her? She had every intention of riding the Grande Roue and, contrary to her earlier thoughts, would prefer not to enjoy Herr Klausman's company as she did it.

She turned her gaze out the window, watching the green fields and great mountains of Bavaria move past. In villages, red-roofed houses clustered around a tall church, while on their outskirts, half-timbered farm buildings with colorful shutters and wooden flower boxes sat among orderly looking fields. Occasionally, the train passed close enough that she could make out the details of a charming scene painted on the white stucco of an outer wall. In the late afternoon, the sun had begun to descend, and the countryside was bathed in a golden glow that made the scene look like a storybook picture.

Frau Maven poked Julia with her elbow and motioned with a lift of her chin at the pile of cards in the center of the table.

It is my turn. Julia brought her thoughts back to the game and studied her cards. She decided to make a safe play, laying down a low card and straightening the pile beneath it. She and Herr Klausman would likely not win this round, but their points would remain steady. Though most took a risk in such games, Julia preferred to take a practical strategy, control what she could, and not make a venture that only might yield an advantage, because of course, in that existed risk of a loss as well.

Nicholas tossed down a card.

Julia did not straighten it on the pile, though she was sorely tempted.

Herr Klausman's brows pulled together for a moment, and he tapped his lip as he studied his hand. "But in spite of the atrocious iron blemish and the formidable wheel, you will love the city of lights, miss." He decided on a card and played it.

A safe play, Julia noted.

"Paris in the springtime—it is marvelous," Herr Klausman continued. "Zeh blossoms, zeh cuisine, zeh art. You will be very pleased with your time there, I think."

"Quite so," Julia replied. "As I mentioned earlier, my grand-mère lives on the Rue—"

"I was very young when I came to Paris for zeh first time. A school lad traveling with my classmates . . ."

Julia frowned and looked at the watch on her wrist and then at the timepiece that hung from a ribbon around her neck. Night would fall soon, and still, five hours and seventeen minutes remained until Strasbourg and, from there, forty-four minutes to Igney-Avricourt. Covering her mouth against a yawn, she considered whether to send for tea. She couldn't afford to fall asleep.

She and Frau Maven would take an early dinner in the restaurant car, and then, with any luck, the older woman would retire for the night. Having her companion safely snoring in her berth was essential to Julia's plan. It was not that she particularly wished to deceive her traveling companion, but if she explained her intention, Frau Maven might forbid her from leaving the train, or worse, she might insist upon accompanying her, which would make the entire venture meaningless. The whole point was for Julia to do it herself. To show her father that she was capable of navigating train stations and reading timetables and traveling alone. She was nearly nineteen years old, after all.

If he would have just listened to her argument, her father would have realized that Julia had traveled more than most young women ever would. She'd visited every art museum in every large city in both Europe and America. She'd even traveled to Toronto and St. Petersburg.

The sound of her companions' voices became more distant, and Julia's chair became more comfortable. The constant rumbling of the engine and the gentle rocking of the train dulled her senses pleasantly.

Another poke from Frau Maven's elbow jolted Julia from her stupor. "Oh, it is my turn again," she muttered, sitting up. She blinked, looking at her cards, then to the stack and back. She set down a card, knowing since she hadn't been watching the game, it had not a chance of being a good play.

"As I was saying, Miss Weston." Herr Klausman's brow furrowed in irritation—understandable, as his partner had nearly fallen asleep in the middle of his story and had played an abominable game. "Paris is a large city. It can be . . . overwhelming. An escort will be very helpful."

"How thoughtful." Frau Maven nodded.

Julia sighed, not bothering to correct him again. "Yes, I do appreciate the offer, Herr Klaus—"

Nicholas coughed loudly, interrupting her. He held his pipe in one hand and covered his mouth with the other, turning slightly so only Julia could see a hint of a smile on his lips. He gave her a small wink, then held up a finger. "A splendid idea, sir. Vith her years of living in zeh city, Miss Veston vould indeed make an excellent tour guide." Nicholas looked at Julia for a moment, his head tipping thoughtfully, then turned back to the confused-looking Herr Klausman. Nicholas then looked at a silver pocket watch and shook his head. "No. Zis vill not do at all," he muttered in a low voice.

Julia wondered if she'd heard him correctly. A strange man indeed.

Nicholas returned the pocket watch to his waistcoat, flipped over a card, and tossed it onto the stack without a glance. "Zaht, I believe is zeh game," he said.

"Oh, well done, sir!" Frau Maven clapped her hands as the pair won again. "You do have a skill for cards."

Nicholas did not respond, as he was already pushing back from the table. He gave a bow, putting on his hat and tipping it to the ladies. "Perhaps you vill join me for a drink and a smoke before dinner, Herr Klausman."

"*Ja*, of course." The other man looked surprised at the sudden termination of the game. He stood, still holding his cards, and bowed to the ladies as well. "I will see you at dinner, then, miss?"

Perhaps when Herr Klausman's mouth was filled with food, Julia might actually have a chance to participate in the conversation. "That would be—" Julia began.

But Nicholas had already turned Herr Klausman around. He took the cards from the man's hand, set them on the table, and then gave him a firm pat on the shoulder that appeared to be more of a push. Herr Klausman turned back once more, but Nicholas, hand still on his shoulder, maneuvered him toward the end of the lounge car. The two walked at a quick pace through the door leading to the next car.

Julia stared after them, trying to understand the reason for the suddenness of the departure. "Nicholas is terribly eccentric, isn't he?" she said to the other woman.

"Such fine men." Frau Maven fidgeted with her scarf, her cheeks pink. She didn't appear to have heard Julia's assessment. She rose. "Come along. We must dress for dinner."

CHAPTER TWO

NEARLY SIX HOURS LATER, JULIA set down her book on the small table beside her berth and put on her wrap. She'd not changed from her evening gown, thinking Frau Maven would be suspicious if she were to discover Julia wearing a different, practical dress so late in the evening. She hadn't changed into her nightclothes, either, not wanting to change twice and risk the noise awakening her companion in the next compartment. She slid her handbag onto her arm and stood still, listening at the door that joined the sleeping compartments.

A mighty snore rumbled from within.

Julia nodded to herself as she checked the timepiece pinned with a ribbon at her waist and her wristwatch. Two minutes. She left the compartment and walked along the outer passageway of the sleeping car until she reached the conductor's seat at the far end next to the door.

"Bonne nuit, mademoiselle." He stood and tipped his hat.

"Bonne nuit, monsieur."

The whistle blew, signaling an approach to the station, and the clacking of the rails grew further apart as the train slowed. Julia thought through her plan again. The Igney-Avricourt station was not as large as others on the route, but the stopover was longer than most.

Taking this same journey a few times per year, Julia and her father had developed a tradition. After dinner, the two would stay up late or, if Julia fell asleep, her father would wake her after Strasbourg. They would disembark at Igney-Avricourt and make their way inside the station to the cart with the old woman named Frau Spreitzer, who according to Julia's father, made the best *gugelhupf* in all of northeastern France.

The whistle blew again, and the lights of the station came into view. As they approached, Julia could see the crowds of people moving beneath the street lamps. Neither the late hour nor the remoteness of the locale prevented the station from being one of the busiest on the line. Frau Spreitzer's cart stand was located in a corner of the station opposite the main doors. Julia had only to walk along the main platform, enter the station, cross through to the far corner, purchase the cake, and then return. The entire endeavor should take less than seven minutes, leaving her at least sixteen until the train departed again. Once she was back in her compartment, she would hide the cake in her valise, change into her bedclothes, and hopefully be exhausted enough to sleep through Frau Maven's snoring. She would wake, refreshed, hours later to the sound of the conductor's knock, thirty minutes before the train arrived in Paris. She nodded to herself. If there was one thing Julia knew, it was how to make and carry out a plan.

The train stopped, and the conductor stepped out to stand at his station beside the door. He took Julia's hand and helped her descend onto the platform.

She glanced at both watches again, appreciating that a train that traveled more than a hundred miles in a day could keep such a precise schedule. *Twenty-three minutes.*

Taking a deep breath, Julia started along through the clouds of steam from the cooling engine toward the main platform, veering around piles of luggage and porters carrying trunks. Families blocked her path here and there, bidding farewell or welcoming a loved one. Voices around her chattered and called out in various languages—some she recognized and others she didn't. She felt conspicuous, dressed as she was in a silk evening gown with feathers in her hair and pearls at her neck. But with the bustling of travelers moving about, she didn't think anyone bothered to notice.

Another train whistled, and a man rushed past, one hand on his bowler hat to prevent it from flying off. Others moved at a more leisurely pace, breathing the night air and stretching their legs between long hours in the confined space of a locomotive.

Julia glanced back, making certain she could see her train among the others stopped at the station. She located it easily, with the familiar gold crest on the side of the cars and the immaculate uniform of the Orient Express conductors stationed at each entry. Reassured that she could find it again, she continued on.

When Julia stepped through the doors into the train station, she found the inside even more crowded than the platforms. Voices and the sound of luggage carts clattering over the brick paving stones echoed off the high ceilings. She didn't remember ever seeing the building so full. But of course, Igney-Avricourt was a main station—a crossroads for quite a few lines—on the way to Paris, which, at this time, would be the most popular destination in the world as people from every nation journeyed to the World's Exposition.

She clutched her handbag closer and pushed her way through the crowd, reaching the far wall and continuing along to the corner of the station. When she arrived at last, the vendor's cart wasn't there. Instead, a row of raised chairs stood against the wall beneath a large sign offering shoe-shining services. Julia would never have imagined anyone to need their shoes shined in the middle of the night, but every chair was filled and other smudged-shoe patrons waited in a queue for their turn.

A pang of disappointment poked in her belly. Had Frau Spreitzer stopped selling her cakes?

Julia looked along the walls, seeing a newspaper stand and, farther on, a man selling cigars from a box attached by straps to his shoulders, but there was no sign of a bakery cart. Glancing in the other direction, she saw only a sea of people in the waiting area.

When she inquired of the cigar salesman, he told her the bakery cart had moved to a new location in the front of the station, near the stagecoach stop.

Julia thanked the cigar man and glanced at both watches. Five minutes had already passed. Tinges of worry started at the disruption to her carefully planned agenda. But quitting now would be foolish—the stop was twenty-three minutes, and if the errand took a few minutes longer than she'd allotted, she would still return to the train with plenty of time to spare. She exited through the doors at the front of the station and relaxed a bit when she inhaled the familiar aroma of the cakes. Following the smell, she found Frau Spreitzer's cart just where the cigar man had said it would be and joined the queue. Thankfully, it was short.

When Frau Spreitzer saw Julia, she grinned, her round cheeks lifting until her eyes were almost completely closed. "Bonne nuit, mademoiselle. You have come for the gugelhupf, no?"

"Oui," Julia said. "Merci."

"But you are alone today." Frau Spreitzer wrapped the cake in paper, speaking French with the unique German accent of the region. "Your father, he remained on the train?"

"I am to meet him in Paris," Julia said, handing a bill to the vendor and accepting her change. Noticing that she was tapping her foot, she stopped.

"Oh, the *Exposition Universelle*." Frau Spreitzer motioned with her chin toward the people moving in and out of the station. "I have never seen such crowds."

"And shall you attend the exposition as well?" Julia put her money carefully into her change purse and closed her handbag.

"Oui, *bien sûr*." Frau Spreitzer handed the cake to Julia, leaning over the cart's top and speaking as if sharing a confidence. "But sadly, this year I will not see Guillaume le Buffle." The older woman raised and lowered her brows. "The American cowboy, he is *très beau*, non?"

"He certainly is," Julia said. Apparently, Buffalo Bill Cody's admirers extended as far as Lorraine, France. A pity he would not be at this year's exposition. His Wild West show had been quite well received eleven years earlier. Julia remembered her father purchasing her an American cowboy hat and introducing her to Annie Oakley. "Merci." She tucked the parcel under her arm and checked the time. Panic flickered in her chest. The train would depart in only eight minutes.

"Enjoy the fair, mademoiselle. And I will see you again, oui? Perhaps in Paris?"

"*Bien sûr. Au revoir*." Julia smiled, then hurried away toward the station doors. She crossed through the indoor waiting area and exited into the steam and confusion of the crowded train platform.

She started toward the train but stopped, feeling unsure as she studied the rows of tracks and the different locomotives. She stepped around a stack of trunks and made her way to the platform where she thought her train waited, but the conductor's uniforms weren't those of the Orient Express staff. Moving back, she walked to the next platform and started along that way.

Again, she didn't recognize the train or the uniformed men standing at the doors to the cars. Had the train moved? Or was she simply turned around? She quickened her pace, hurrying back toward the station to find a platform attendant.

Stepping back around the stack of trunks, she nearly bumped into a pair of men. A wave of relief flowed over her when she recognized the one in a black coat. She hadn't seen Nicholas since before dinner, and even then, it was only very briefly. Herr Klausman had been walking toward the table where she and Frau Maven sat in the restaurant cart when Nicholas had caught up to him, stopping him and introducing him to the diners at a different table, then joining him. Herr Klausman had glanced Julia's way throughout the meal with an apologetic expression, but she had left before his dinner was finished. Frau Maven had been extremely disappointed to miss out on the gentlemen's company and had voiced her displeasure continually, ruining what should have been a splendid dinner. Julia always looked forward to the meals on the Orient Express. The cuisine was created by world-renowned chefs and served on sparkling china and crisp white linens with artistically folded napkins. One could not dress too formally, and watching the parade of the most fashionable attire from various countries had always been a favorite part of the journey.

She had been more than happy to bid the woman good night and retire to her own compartment.

"Monsieur Nicholas," Julia said. "Thank goodness. Please, can you tell me—?"

"Mademoiselle Weston." Nicholas's eyes lit up, and he removed his pipe. "Zeh very person I hoped to see." He stepped to the side and motioned to his companion. "You must meet *mon bon ami*, Monsieur Luc Paquet."

"Bonjour, Monsieur Paquet." Julia kept her voice polite but couldn't help but glance back toward the trains.

Nicholas hung the pipe back in his mouth and held out his other hand toward Julia with a flourish. "And here we have zeh delightful Mademoiselle Julia Weston."

Monsieur Paquet pulled off his hat to reveal a head of dark-blond hair. He bowed. *"Un plaisir de vous rencontrer, mademoiselle."*

Julia determined immediately that M. Paquet was French but not Parisian. His accent was rural, as were his manners—the deep bow was rather old-fashioned, as was the greeting. What could a gentleman such as Nicholas possibly have in common with a man with such a low social status?

Monsieur Paquet lifted his gaze to hers. Deep brown eyes surrounded by dark lashes looked into her own. The color was surprisingly warm, and just for a moment, she stared.

At that instant, a puff of smoke came from Nicholas's pipe, filling the air with a lavender scent.

Julia shook her head, thinking her worry and lack of sleep must have her imagining things. Pipe smoke didn't smell like lavender. And she was nearly certain Nicholas's pipe hadn't been lit.

"Monsieur Paquet returns to Provence from Athens," Nicholas said.

"How nice." Julia looked back at the trains again, pulling her wrap tighter around her shoulders and shifting the cake into her other arm.

"He brings a shipment of olive cuttings for his orchard," Nicholas continued.

"Ah," Julia said, willing herself not to check the time again. "I see."

Monsieur Paquet's gaze flicked to the feathers in her hair. And though the politeness never left his expression, Julia got the impression he thought her attire ridiculous for a train station.

Heat moved up her neck, and she lifted her chin. She didn't give one fig about this rustic's opinion of her appearance. His faded trousers were wrinkled, his bouclé coat worn, and his thick boots could benefit immensely from a few moments at Igney-Avricourt's new shoe-shining booth. A tickle of guilt wiggled in her stomach at her unkind thoughts, but Julia's worry over missing her train overrode any remorse for the harsh judgment.

"Nicholas, I'm afraid I'm rather lost," Julia said. "Can you show me to the right train?"

The man in black turned fully toward her, tipping his head and taking his pipe out of his mouth with a slow movement as he considered her. "Sometimes zeh right train is not zeh right train, eh?" He glanced at his silver pocket watch, closing it with a snap.

Frustration and worry tightened her chest. She had no time for riddles. The train would depart at any moment. "Please, sir. I must hurry."

"Come along, zen, mademoiselle." Nicholas offered his arm, tipping his hat in farewell to the other man. "I shall see you safely aboard."

"Thank you." She took his arm. "Au revoir, Monsieur Paquet."

"Au revoir, Mademoiselle Weston."

Julia allowed herself to be led along a smoky platform to the stairs leading onto the train. The conductor was apparently helping another passenger, so Nicholas assisted her as she climbed aboard.

Now that her worry had abated, exhaustion took its place, leaving her more tired than she'd been before. "Merci, Nicholas," Julia spoke through a yawn. "I'm afraid I was quite lost for a moment."

He looked up at her from the platform and tipped his black hat. "As we say in my country, 'Sometimes one must lose himself to find himself.'" He chuckled as if he'd told a joke. "Or in zis case, *her*self. Au revoir, mademoiselle."

"Au revoir." Julia yawned again. She walked along the darkened corridor and retired to her sleeping compartment for the night, so pleased with her accomplishment that Frau Maven's snores didn't bother her at all.

CHAPTER THREE

JULIA HEARD A VOICE OUTSIDE her compartment door. "*On arrive!*" the conductor called, moving down the passageway.

She rolled over, stretched, and winced at the tightness of her bodice. She must have fallen asleep in her gown last night, something she'd never done before. The very idea of not hanging the dress properly in her closet and changing into the nightgown she'd carefully laid out was utterly unaccepta—

She looked around the sleeping compartment, registering what she was seeing, and all thoughts on garment care halted abruptly. She sat up. The deep mahogany wood and velvet curtains had been replaced by durable-looking benches and window blinds. The porcelain basin and its stand were gone altogether, as were Julia's clothes and luggage. Her cake sat on a small wooden table attached beneath the windowsill.

Now fully awake, she jumped up from the berth. Surely, she couldn't be in the wrong compartment. *Impossible.* But there was no mistaking the disparity in her surroundings. This was clearly not a first-class sleeping car on a luxury train.

How could this have happened?

She forced herself to take a breath, sit down, and think through the situation rationally. Last evening she'd boarded the train, bid good night to Nicholas, and then . . .

Then what? She blinked, trying to remember. After leaving Nicholas, her memory was fuzzy. She remembered moving down the corridor, and she must have found her compartment number on the door. But in her sleepy state and impaired by darkness, she hadn't realized she was in the wrong car. What other explanation could there be?

Her predicament was embarrassing but easily corrected. She'd have to walk through the train in her wrinkled gown with squashed feathers in her hair to her real sleeping compartment. But with any luck, most of the other passengers would be busy in their own quarters, preparing to disembark in Paris. She looked at both of her watches, noting that she'd been woken later than usual. *Much* later. Had the train been delayed? Her father would not be pleased at having to wait for hours at the Paris station.

She needed to return to her compartment quickly to change her clothes, hopefully before Frau Maven realized her charge had slept in a different part of the train.

A new thought brought an odd mixture of horror and relief. What if the compartment had been occupied when Julia had blindly stumbled inside?

She hung her wrap over her arm with her handbag, picked up the cake, and left the compartment, chuckling to herself as she imagined the catastrophe she'd narrowly avoided.

The laughter died on her lips, however, when she came to the door separating the train cars and a conductor stepped into the passageway, blocking her path. He looked down a long thin nose, beneath which a bushy straw-colored mustache twitched. "*S'il vous plaît, mademoiselle.* Passengers are not permitted in the baggage car."

The baggage car? But the first-class carriage was directly behind the baggage car. She blinked again, glancing out the window to determine the train's direction and trying to comprehend how she'd become so disoriented. "I'm returning to my compartment, if you please," she told the conductor, doing her best to stand tall, despite how silly she knew she must look. "In the first-class car."

The conductor glanced back at the compartment she'd come out of, raising his bushy brows. "The PLM Railway has no first-class car, mademoiselle. Perhaps you are confused. Too much to drink last evening, eh?" He looked pointedly at the smashed feathers and the cake.

"No, I . . ." Julia's words trailed off as cold filled her insides. "What did you say? The *PLM* Railway?" She looked back out the window. Instead of the green rolling hills and the blue Marne River overhung with lush willows, the view was of tall rocky mountains with scrubby-looking trees. On a distant hill, she could make out a stone city surrounded by a wall. Pulling her gaze back to the conductor, she realized he didn't wear the brass-buttoned uniform of a Wagons Lit conductor but a gray coat and a hat with an unfamiliar symbol. The chill spread, tingeing her thoughts with panic.

"Sir." She grabbed on to his arm, choking on her words. "Where am I?"

"We left Montélimar perhaps an hour and a half ago, mademoiselle."

"Provence?" Julia released the man's arm, feeling lightheaded as the truth of the situation settled over her. *No, no, no. This can't be happening.* She'd traveled hundreds of miles in the wrong direction. She looked at her watch, then the pocket watch that hung at her waist. Her father and grand-mère would have met the train—the right train—hours earlier. They must be frantic with worry. She leaned against the wall of the corridor, feeling faint, her thoughts rushing in every direction as she tried to make sense of the situation.

"Mademoiselle, you are unwell?"

"I must send a telegram to my father right away." She moved closer to the window, looking down the tracks in hopes of seeing a city. "I was expected hours ago in Paris. He will be sick with worry."

"Paris?" The conductor shook his head and made a tutting noise. "Oh la la, you are very far from home." He held out a hand, urging her to return back along the corridor. "Come along, mademoiselle. Return to your compartment and rest. I will bring something to calm you."

Julia didn't move. An ache had started in her head, and she rubbed at it absently. "That is not my compartment."

He moved closer, as if to herd her in the direction he wanted her to go. "Mademoiselle, you are confused and—"

The train's whistle cut his words short.

The sound firmed Julia's resolve. She drew herself up, standing tall. This was not the time to fall apart. She was perfectly capable of managing a small miscalculation. The train slowed, nearing its next stop. She would simply disembark and, at the station, find a timetable, purchase a new ticket, and send a telegram to her father. Thank goodness for the cash in her handbag. Within a few hours, she would be on her way to Paris, and tonight, she and her family would laugh about the *erreur* over a slice of gugelhupf. "I am not confused, thank you," she told the conductor in a much calmer voice.

The twitch of his mustache indicated he wasn't entirely convinced, but he moved away to his post by the door in preparation for the train's arrival at the station.

The train continued to slow, and Julia saw a sign. *Rivulet.* She'd never heard of it, but it was as good a place as any, she reasoned. Provence was out of her way, but the world would not end. Her only disappointment was to miss out on a day at the World's Exhibition.

Once the train stopped, Julia moved to the door.

The bushy-mustached conductor climbed out and took her hand. "Your luggage, mademoiselle?"

"I have none," she said, stepping down and ignoring his brow lift.

"Very well, mademoiselle."

The morning was misty, and dark clouds hung heavy in the sky, portending rain. Julia pulled her wrap tighter and shivered, wishing she had a coat. The wrap was elegant, well-suited to a dinner on a heated train, but it offered no protection from the chilly, cloudy morning. She started toward the small stone building that served as Rivulet's train station, thinking she should get inside before the rain began.

The station's entrance was located on the far side of the building, opposite the train tracks but facing the road. She supposed the building predated the railway, and nobody had bothered to change it for convenience of the train travelers.

The door was locked.

Julia knocked and stepped to the side to look through a window. She cupped her hand against the glass and peered close but could see nobody within. A small plaque was on the desk, bearing the name, *Mathieu Laurent*. He must be the stationmaster.

She looked up the road in both directions but saw no structures. Aside from a horse in a paddock beside the station, there was no sign of life. Where was the town? A shiver that had nothing to do with the chilly morning moved over her skin.

The train whistled, and she could hear it start away.

Well, perhaps the stationmaster was simply in a back room. She looked through other windows, moving around the side of the building. When she reached the back of the station again, she noticed two large crates beside the tracks—those had certainly not been there a moment earlier—and recognized Greek lettering painted on the sides, though she couldn't read it.

The smoke from the train's coal and the caboose of the receding locomotive as it picked up speed gave her a moment of panic; she feared she'd been too hasty disembarking in an unknown place. But the stationmaster must return soon, she reasoned. Better to wait here than to continue on, getting farther away from her destination.

Hearing a horse's whinny, she turned and saw the man Nicholas had introduced her to at the Igney-Avricourt station. *Luc Paquet,* she remembered. It stood to reason that the countryman lived in this desolate location. She felt both relief at seeing a familiar face and frustration that the only other person in this place was the critical rustic. He was leading the horse from the paddock to a wagon beside the road.

Julia blew out a breath and approached him. "Bonjour, Monsieur Paquet."

He glanced up and returned to attaching the horse's harness. "Mademoiselle."

The horse bobbed its head, and Julia stepped back, wary. The animal was large and sturdy-looking, nothing like the sleek carriage horses she was used to. And what if it should want to eat her cake?

"At what time does the station open?" She checked both of her watches, wanting to be certain they were in accord. She could not afford to miss the train to Paris.

"Maybe after lunch. Maybe later." Monsieur Paquet tugged a worn leather strap, feeding it through its buckle. He didn't look at her as he pulled the strap tight and patted the horse's neck. "Today is Monday. It might not open at all."

Julia had not previously heard the man speak more than a greeting, and for a moment his words were almost impossible to understand with the thick Provençal pronunciation. A moment passed before she comprehended completely what he'd said.

By the time she did, he was walking back around the station.

Julia followed. She didn't appreciate his teasing. A civil servant didn't simply choose whether he was inclined to work or not. Trains ran on schedules and followed rules. "*Excusez-moi.* I must speak to the stationmaster. I need to purchase a ticket. And to send a telegram. You see, I'm supposed to be in Paris."

"You're a long way from Paris." He hefted one of the crates with a grunt.

"Yes, I know." She followed him back to the wagon, forcing her feet not to stomp in frustration and keeping her voice polite. "My father will be very worried. From whence might I send a telegram?"

"Nowhere around here." He lifted the crate into the wagon. "Nearest place is Beaucaire, about thirty miles that way." He motioned up the road with his chin, then started back around the station.

Thunder sounded overhead as Julia looked in the direction he'd indicated. Surely he wasn't suggesting she walk thirty miles along a dirt road in her evening gown. Could she hire a carriage? But where? Raindrops started to fall.

Monsieur Paquet pushed the second crate into the wagon and lifted up the back gate and secured it closed.

Julia shifted the cake to her other arm and pulled her wrap tighter. "I am sure the stationmaster will return and open the door once he sees the rain. I shall wait perfectly comfortably inside."

"Wait for what?" He pulled a sheet of canvas over the crates and started to tie it down.

"Why, the next train, of course. Surely it won't be too long. Good day, monsieur." Julia turned and started back to the station. A small bench sat next to the door beneath a section of overhanging roof, where she could at least be dry. She would wait there.

"Next train comes through on Friday." Monsieur Paquet spoke from behind her before she reached the bench.

She whirled. "Friday? You can't be serious."

He shrugged.

A tightness constricted her throat. "But I can't . . . What will I do?" Tears threatened, and she turned back toward the bench, not wanting him to see her distress. Rain now poured down, and she hurried to the station door, pounding on it again before her last shred of hope dissipated and she sat down on the bench.

Could this man possibly be telling the truth? She couldn't believe it. But what if he were? Despite her attempts to think through the situation rationally, despair crowded out every thought, and her tears started in earnest. *What am I to do?* She buried her face in her hands, feeling sick with discouragement. *Father will be so worried*, she thought. And disappointed. *Now I shall never travel anywhere without a chaperone. And what if the stationmaster doesn't come?*

The toes of two scuffed boots moved into her line of vision.

Julia jerked up her head, wiping away her tears and trying to hold her composure while Monsieur Paquet stood before her.

He moved closer, ducking beneath the overhang, and held out his coat to her. "Come along, then."

His voice was not unkind, but of course she couldn't trust a man she'd just met. "Where are we going?"

"Do you intend to sit here in the rain for five days?"

Julia took a handkerchief from her handbag and wiped under her nose, trying to regain her composure. "I can't go with you. You could be a . . . a man of poor character." She lifted her chin, daring him to deny it.

He gave a flat stare, though his lips twitched. "I am not a man of poor character."

"That is exactly what a man of poor character would say." She returned the handkerchief and closed her handbag with a snap, having proved her point.

"Mademoiselle, I will take you to my aunt's house. Tante Gabrielle is always pleased to have company." He glanced back at the wagon. "Unless you prefer to remain here until Friday."

The mocking in his tone spurred her anger. Julia opened her mouth to argue. How could she be certain he had an aunt? Wasn't this precisely the sort of scenario that led to young women being kidnapped and kept as prisoners in an evil prince's dungeon? And even more than her fear of capture was her frustration at having to be rescued from her own mistake.

M. Paquet frowned, folding his arms around the coat. "Mademoiselle Weston, I have no wish to stand in the rain arguing. You and your cake can either get in the wagon or stay here until Friday. *Je m'en fiche.*"

Julia hesitated. What choice did she have? The stationmaster may or may not return for days. And even if he did, she had no assurance that he would find her lodgings until the train came. If there were even lodgings to be had in this place. She studied Monsieur Paquet for a moment. This scruffy rustic scowling at her was the only person she knew for hundreds of miles and the only person who'd offered to assist her in her predicament. She had no alternative but to trust him.

"Very well, monsieur. I shall accompany you." Julia took the offered coat and slid her bare arms into the scratchy sleeves, immediately grateful for their warmth. "But I'll reimburse your aunt, of course. I do not wish to impose on her hospitality."

His flat look held, and he looked as if he might scoff. He started off into the rain toward the wagon, pulling his hat low over his brow.

His dismissiveness only served to irritate Julia further. She would be very pleased once she was safely installed at Tante Gabrielle's house and rid of Luc Paquet.

CHAPTER FOUR

THE WAGON SEAT WAS HARD, and the road was bumpy. Julia was, in a word, miserable. She held on to the bench with one hand and M. Paquet's coat tightly at her neck with the other, glad M. Pacquet had placed the cake in the wagon so she could have her hands free to keep herself firmly in her seat. The rain continued to pour down steadily, and after a while, tired of drops running down her neck, she pulled the thick coat up over her head, deciding her feather arrangement was most likely ruined anyway. The coat did little to keep her dry, and she wondered if she would be warmer without it now that it was soaked through, but she thought M. Paquet's gesture in offering it to her was nice. So she kept it. At least it kept the rain from dribbling over her bare shoulders and down her back.

The pair continued along in silence, and as she watched the scenery go past, Julia became more certain with every moment that she'd made the right choice. The area was very remote. She looked at her watches. The wagon hadn't passed a single house in nearly an hour since they'd left the station. If she'd remained and the stationmaster hadn't come, she was certain she'd not have found a place to stay. What would she have done when night fell? Slept on the bench outside the train station? The idea was terrifying.

She glanced at her companion. M. Paquet rode with shoulders hunched and his head low, occasionally tipping his head forward to let the water run off his hat brim and splash between his boots. He wore a brown vest buttoned up over his loose cotton shirt and no necktie. She wondered if the brim of his hat was sufficient to keep water from trickling down his collar. Probably not. The man didn't seem particularly comfortable in the rain but rather resigned to it. Julia supposed when one worked out of doors, one became used to inclement weather.

"How is it that you are here in Provence instead of Paris, mademoiselle?" The man's voice came out as a grumble.

She shifted around in the seat to face him. "I boarded the wrong train in Igney-Avricourt, if you must know. I was supposed to be on the Orient Express."

He turned to look at her, his brows raised until they disappeared beneath his hat brim. "You mistook a PLM Railway train for the Orient Express?"

"It was your friend Nicholas," Julia said, feeling extremely defensive. "He delivered me to the wrong train."

"He is not my friend." M. Paquet turned back to watch the road ahead.

"But he said you are his 'bon ami,'" Julia reminded him.

"I had only met him a moment before you arrived," he said, shrugging. "He did act as though he knew me. He did not put *me* onto the wrong train, however."

"I don't understand," Julia said. "What sort of man . . . ? Surely he made a mistake. Didn't he? He is not the type to purposely deceive. Or, at least, he didn't seem to be."

"*Je ne sais pas.*" M. Paquet shrugged again. "As I said, I spoke to him only for a short moment."

In all the confusion of the day, this was the first time Julia had truly considered how she'd come to be in this mess in the first place. Now that she had time to think, she didn't know whether to be furious with Nicholas or feel sorry for him. He may have been confused and missed his train as well. But if he had intentionally led her to the wrong train, she couldn't begin to comprehend why he would possibly do such a thing. "If he acted deliberately, what reason might he have for misdirecting me so?" she asked.

"How is it that you didn't notice the error immediately?" he asked in return.

How hadn't she? "Well, I was very tired, I suppose." Julia thought back to the night before. "And a bit disoriented. Did you think Nicholas's pipe smoke smelled like lavender?"

He glanced at her. "Pipe smoke doesn't smell like lavender."

She realized his answer wasn't a denial, but he spoke before she could ask again.

"What was a young lady such as yourself doing alone on a train anyway?"

Julia bristled at the question. She sat up straight and let the coat fall from her head, and she wished she looked dignified instead of wet when it plopped onto her shoulders. "Monsieur, I am perfectly capable of traveling alone."

He cut a glance at her.

Her stomach clenched at his unspoken observation. "Well, usually—when a person doesn't give me false directions." She huffed, pulling the soggy coat tight around her neck. "Besides, I wasn't alone. I had a traveling companion, Frau Maven."

"And where was this Frau Maven while you were wandering about a crowded station in the middle of the night?"

"She was asleep," Julia said. "You see, I wanted to purchase a cake for my father." She motioned toward the bed of the wagon, where M. Paquet had placed the parcel beneath the canvas with her handbag. "That is why I left my train." She turned back and looked down at the ruined silk of her fanciest shoes, the discouragement of her failure feeling heavy like the wet coat. "And now I am here, in this . . . place."

"It isn't the worst place," Monsieur Paquet said in a low voice. His tone suggested she may have offended him.

Julia winced at her own bluntness and hurried to soften it. "Oh, I'm sure you appreciate it. It's your home, after all. But you see, I am meant to be in a city surrounded by music and theater and art and—"

"And you don't believe any of that exists here."

His tone hadn't changed.

"I . . . well, I assumed . . ." She decided a change of subject was in order. "Where is *here*, anyway? The sign at the station said *Rivulet*, but I didn't see a town. Is it in the other direction?"

M. Paquet shook his head. "Riv is very small. Just a few families. It is more of a hamlet, really."

"That is why the train doesn't stop daily," she said.

"Oui. We are simple people here, tending our farms. Most of us do not travel at all and the rest rarely." He pushed back the brim of his hat, glancing upward, and Julia noticed the downpour had lessened to a drizzle.

"I travel quite a bit." Julia kept talking to avoid another awkward silence. "With my father. He serves as the Great Britain Commissioner for Fine Arts."

M. Paquet turned toward her quickly, looking as if he would say something but then thought better of it. He faced back toward the road. "Ah, that explains your accent. You are English."

"*Half* English." *And I'm not the one with an accent.* "My mother was Parisian."

"You live in Paris?"

"I live in Vienna now. I instruct at a young lady's finishing school. I return on holidays and during the summer to stay with my grand-mère, and my father meets me. But this year, instead of traveling to view the work of a new artist he's discovered or oversee the purchase of a masterpiece for a museum, he is responsible for organizing the collection of artwork that will be displayed at the World's Fair. From what he tells me, the British artists have quite a prospect of earning medals. And France has a marvelous showing as well, but of course, that is to be expected."

M. Paquet had gone very silent, and she realized that she was speaking of a subject that could not possibly interest him. Of course a simple countryman was not concerned with the world of international fine art.

"But I am rambling, and I don't suppose such a thing is interesting to you," she said.

Instead of answering, he glanced at her, then pointed ahead.

Julia squinted through the rain, and a house came into view. A low peach-and-gray stone wall ran along the road beneath a large almond tree covered in pink blossoms. The house was two stories, built of the same stone, and sitting at the end of a path that began at a break in the wall.

M. Paquet drew the wagon to a halt. "Tante Gabrielle's house." He helped Julia from the wagon and fetched her cake and handbag from the rear of the wagon before leading her up the garden path.

The house was charming, in a primitive sort of way. The shutters next to the windows were painted a bright sky blue, and ivy grew over the outer walls. Mismatched flowerpots filled with a variety of blossoms sat on windowsills and along the ground beneath them.

Another house sat nearby on the same side of the road, and through the sprinkling rain, Julia could see at least one other farther along.

When they drew near, the door flung open, and a slender woman wearing a homespun dress and apron stepped out, spreading her arms wide. "Luc, you've returned!" Black and gray curls escaped the scarf tied around her hair, flying around her face. She drew him into an embrace, kissing both his cheeks. "How I've missed you, *mon cher*." She pulled back, holding him at arm's length. "And you are soaked through. Come inside."

If Julia had considered M. Paquet's accent to be strong, that was nothing to his aunt's. The sounds managed to be both guttural and nasal, and it seemed as though a random vowel might be thrown into the sentence at any time. She found it nearly impossible to understand without extreme concentration.

"Gabi, I've brought a guest." M. Paquet stepped to the side, allowing his aunt to see past him. "This is Mademoiselle Julia Weston. Mademoiselle Weston, meet my aunt, Gabrielle Martin."

"*Un plaisir,*" Julia said.

When her gaze landed on Julia, Gabrielle Martin's eyes went wide. "Oh, *ma chérie,* you must be frozen through. Come inside right away." She took Julia's arm and pulled her through the doorway, tutting as she helped Julia remove the wet coat. "This dress is not suitable for such weather." She shook her head. "You look like a dog who fell into the pond. Stay here. I will bring towels." She rushed up a flight of stairs.

"*Je suis désolé,*" Monsieur Paquet grimaced. "My aunt speaks without thinking. You do not look like a wet dog, mademoiselle."

"I certainly feel like one," Julia said. She turned around to view the entryway, noticing a small parlor on the other side of the stairs.

The woodwork was dark, the walls whitewashed plaster, and the floor stone. A pile of boots and shoes was heaped under a bench next to the door. A row of hooks held coats and hats. On the wall across from the front door, books, a few dirty dishes, and more flowerpots cluttered the sidebar table. Above it, in a simple frame . . .

"Oh my," Julia said. She moved closer to study the painting.

The scene was rendered in the impressionist style, a new movement popularized by such masters as Gaugin and Monet. It depicted a country house—the very one in which she stood, based on its almond tree, blue shutters, and flowerpots. Light played over the stones of the house and wall, adding movement and depth. In the shadows beneath the tree she could make out two figures sitting, perhaps enjoying a picnic, and beyond, orchards and lavender fields stretched toward mountains shrouded in mist. The painting was reminiscent of a dream or a memory, perfectly capturing the essence of impressionism. And although it was clearly created by someone with an exceptional grasp of composition, Julia was certain the artist was not one she'd seen before. There was something incredibly distinct about the style. It gave a sense of longing that touched a very personal place inside her soul.

"Who is the artist?" She didn't take her eyes from the painting as she spoke. "This is exceptional."

"It is no one you've heard of," Luc said.

Julia turned toward him. "This should be displayed at l'Exposition Universelle. Is the artist local? I must meet him. Or her."

Monsieur Paquet didn't answer. He looked up to where his aunt was bringing down an armful of towels and hurried up the steps to assist her.

A moment later, a towel was wrapped around Julia's shoulders, another around her wet hair, and she sat in a soft chair before the kitchen hearth, a black-and-white cat weaving around her legs.

Monsieur Paquet had a towel around his shoulders as well, and a tabby cat on his lap. He sat at a kitchen table that was covered with dishes, laundry, and even more flowerpots and looked through the window above the washbasin.

"Thank you, Madame Martin," Julia said, accepting a mug of tea.

"Oh, none of this 'madame' business." She swatted her hand in the air as if to hit the word out of the room. "I am Gabi to my friends." She pushed aside a pile of linens and set a mug on the table in front of her nephew. "And to my enemies, I suppose," she added thoughtfully. "Now, Juliette, tell me how you found yourself in Riv, dressed in an evening gown in the pouring rain."

The French version of her name reminded Julia of her grandmother.

Gabi took a seat on the other side of the hearth. "I imagine the tale involves a handsome gentleman and perhaps some romantic intrigue, oui?" She raised and lowered her brows a few times.

Monsieur Paquet snorted.

"I'm afraid not," Julia said, hiding a smile at the older woman's insinuation. "I was supposed to go to Paris, but I boarded the wrong train and found myself stranded in Rivulet by accident. Monsieur Paquet was kind enough to help me."

"*Voilà!*" Gabi held up a finger. "A handsome gentleman." She turned her finger to point toward the kitchen table.

"Ah, oui." Julia's cheeks went hot, and she kept her gaze from the other side of the kitchen. "He is . . . handsome."

Julia could feel M. Paquet's embarrassment, though he made no sound. She didn't dare look in his direction.

"And you are meant to be in Paris?" Gabi said, continuing as if she hadn't noticed any discomfort. "Your family must be worried when you did not arrive."

Julia took a sip of her tea and nodded. "I'd hoped to send a telegram, but apparently that is not possible. Perhaps I could send word by mail. If I post a letter today, when will it arrive in Paris?"

Gabi made the tutting sound again. "The mail isn't due today. And you never know. It may not come tomorrow either, if Jacques Dubois is distracted in Madeline Auclair's Taverne." She leaned close and waggled her brows again. "Or by Mademoiselle Auclair herself."

At this rate, the heat in Julia's cheeks would never have a chance to dissipate. And the frustration of being unable to contact her family remained. "Does nothing in Provence run on a schedule?" she asked.

"A visit to the privy precisely one hour after my morning coffee," Gabi said, laughing. "*That* you can set your clock by." She glanced toward the window. "The mistral winds are regular as well, blowing like the devil himself wanted to freeze Provence in the spring." Her eyes twinkled. "And then, nine months later, you can always count on a busy schedule for the midwife."

Shocked at the lady's indelicacy, Julia drew in a quick breath, touching her fingers to her lips.

"Gabi," Monsieur Paquet interjected. He looked as if he were holding back a smile. "I do not think Mademoiselle Weston expected an answer to her question."

Gabi winked at Julia, then laughed. "Those are the questions I prefer to answer most of all."

CHAPTER FIVE

JULIA SAT BACK IN THE chair, savoring the warmth of her tea. Gabi was definitely an original; she was a person apparently unconcerned with topics appropriate for a first meeting. But somehow her candor set Julia at ease and made her feel welcome in the most unwelcoming of circumstances.

Luc finished his tea and lifted the tabby cat as he stood, then set the animal back to curl up on his chair before he left to care for the horse.

Gabi stood, taking the empty tea mug from Julia and setting it on the mantel with her own next to a cracked vase, a framed photograph of a baby, and an apparently forgotten piece of bread. "Come along, Juliette. You will be wanting to change into dry clothes and take a warm bath, oui?"

"Merci." Julia stood as well. She handed the wet towels to her hostess, who hung them over the kitchen chairs, and stepping carefully over the black-and-white cat, she followed Gabi up the stairs. As she passed the painting in the front corridor, she paused, but since Gabi had already started up the stairs, Julia made a note to ask again about the artist once she was settled. Her father would be very pleased that she'd discovered an unknown talent. Maybe the unintended detour to Provence would not be a complete waste.

Gabi paused on the landing at the top of the stairs. "I typically put guests in the Sunflower Room. It has the best view of the mountains." She tapped a door but did not open it. "But Luc is in that room now, so you will have to make do with the other." She turned and opened the door directly across the corridor. "Voilá. The Lavender Room."

Julia followed her inside and smiled. Gabi certainly knew how to adhere to a theme. The walls were painted a lovely pale lavender shade. A bed with a wrought-iron frame and light-purple bedding stood on one side of the room, a washstand and a wardrobe painted in the same color on the other. A portrait of a lavender field in full bloom hung over the washstand. Julia studied it for a moment. It was beautiful, but she could tell immediately the artist was not the same as the one who'd painted the scene in the front hall.

Gabi pulled the sheer curtains to the side and pushed up the window sash. The sweet, subtle scent of almond blossoms filled the room.

Julia stepped to the window to admire the tree, thinking she had rarely had such a lovely view during her travels. "It's perfect," she said.

Gabi smiled. "This was my daughter's room." She picked up a book from the floor and a shawl that hung over the back of the desk chair. "Her favorite color was . . ." She spread her arms, indicating the room around them.

"Lavender," Julia finished, unsure of what to say. Had Gabi lost her daughter? "How old was she?" She asked the question softly, her voice filled with the compassion she considered appropriate.

"Oh dear. I made it sound like Suzette died, didn't I?" Gabi said, laughing. "She is alive and well and living in Lyon with her husband. Both of my children have moved away. They all do." She glanced toward the window. "But not Luc. He is determined to carry on the family legacy."

"The olive orchard?" Julia asked.

"Oui." Gabi nodded, looking more somber than she had since Julia arrived. "He feels a responsibility to his late father—my brother." She sighed and gave an affectionate smile. "Loyalty and stubbornness with a dash of sentimentality. That is the character of *le garçon*."

"Gabi, this is so very kind of you, and I fully intend to reimburse you for your hospitality." A breeze blew through the window, reminding Julia that she was still wearing wet clothing. She shivered.

"That is not necessary at all, ma chérie." Gabi opened the purple wardrobe, revealing a mirror on the inside of the door and hangers full of clothing. She tossed the book and shawl inside. "And it is not the Provençal way. I will not accept money for taking in a guest. It is a privilege."

"Then, I will find a way to repay you. I can do chores to earn my keep."

"I will not turn away help. Heaven knows I could use it." Gabi looked Julia up and down for a moment, then pulled out a few articles of clothing. "Here. These should fit nicely. And I'm sure there are boots or shoes in your size downstairs by the front door." She laid the clothes on the bed. "But I'm afraid my underclothing would not fit you. Not without some padding." She chuckled at her joke.

"I can manage with my own . . . unmentionables," Julia stuttered, embarrassment making her words tumble over one another.

"The washroom is there, next to your room." Gabi pointed at the wall. "And across from it is my own bedchamber. I call it the Peony Room." She closed the wardrobe and moved to the doorway. "Lunch will be ready when you are. Please, make yourself at home."

"Merci."

Julia examined her reflection in the purple wardrobe mirror. She wore a full, heavy skirt in a rust color with a collarless white-linen blouse. A blue garment that appeared to be a cross between a gentleman's waistcoat and a corset was pulled tight over the blouse, and an apron tied around her waist completed the ensemble. She put on her wristwatch and hung the other timepiece around her neck.

Instead of wrapping her hair in the scarf Gabi had left, Julia left it loose to dry, glad to have a chance to comb it. The feathered headpiece was a soggy, crushed mess, and by the time she'd unpinned it, it was so ruined that she'd tossed it into the wastebasket and brushed the leaves and dried blossoms from the windowsill into the receptacle for good measure. Gabi was a warm and generous hostess, but a fastidious housekeeper she was not.

The tabby cat brushed at her legs, and Julia crouched down to pet it. The animal had been in the Lavender Room when Julia had returned from her bath and had curled up on the bed to nap while she'd dressed.

The washroom was surprisingly well equipped with a basin tub, warm water from the faucet, and even an adjoining water closet. Julia hadn't expected such conveniences in the rural location and was immensely grateful not to have had to heat and haul her water or use an outdoor privy as her grand-mére often reminded her was the way when she was young.

Feeling satisfied at being clean and dry, Julia picked up the cat and left the bedchamber. The door to the Sunflower Room was still closed, and Julia could not help her curiosity at what the room must look like. Was it entirely yellow, as she imagined, with sunny walls and daffodil-colored furniture?

But considering M. Paquet's room brought to mind the man himself, and Julia did not think it proper to think of him in such a personal space. The idea of his bedchamber so near to hers was unsettling. She tried to tell herself it was no different than sleeping in neighboring compartments on a train, but being inside a home was different and somehow more intimate. What if the two should meet in the corridor in their nightclothes on the way to the water closet? The burning in her face she'd felt so often since entering Gabi's house came back in full force, and she took a moment to compose herself before going downstairs.

"Oh, you found Fredric." Gabi was cutting a loaf of warm bread into thick slices. "That one—he is always making friends." She pointed at the cat with the knife. "You look much better, Juliette, now that you are no longer wet and shivering."

The sight and smell of the food made Julia's stomach rumble. She set down the cat and took the seat Gabi indicated.

"I hope you like *soupe au pistou*." Gabi ladled soup into two bowls, then rummaged around in one drawer and another before she produced two spoons and joined Julia.

"It smells delicious," Julia said.

"Go on, then." Gabi motioned with her spoon. "*Bon appétit*."

"Shall we not wait for Monsieur Paquet?" Julia asked.

"Luc ate and left quickly. He doesn't believe he'll return before nightfall. Apparently an important errand. Je ne sais pas." Gabi shrugged and spread butter over her bread.

Julia felt a bit of disappointment, thinking she might have liked for M. Paquet to see her in a dry gown she hadn't slept in without a mass of soggy feathers in her hair. She took a slice of the dark-colored bread, surprised by how heavy it felt. Following Gabi's lead, she spread butter over it and took a bite. The bread had a thick crust and was very chewy. Nothing at all like the light baguettes Paris bakers prided themselves on.

She took a tentative bite of the soup, recognizing pasta, potatoes, and vegetables, but she wasn't prepared for the burst of basil flavoring. The country food was hearty and delicious, especially after a long wet morning. Before she knew it, the soup was gone, and in spite of Julia's protests, Gabi ladled more into her bowl and gave her another piece of bread.

"You must try *le fromage de chèvre* as well." She offered a plate with triangles of a pungent cream-colored cheese.

Julia took a small bite, surprised by its creamy sweetness. "It is very good."

"It is Coquette, my new goat," Gabi said proudly. "Every year, Madame Laurent's chèvre wins first place at the Fête du Fromage." She scowled in the direction of her neighbor's house. "But not this year. No more second place." She pointed to the cheese. "Coquette's milk is the sweetest in all of Provence, and in a few weeks, I will triumph at last." She raised a finger into the air dramatically.

"With this chèvre, you will surely win." Julia smiled at the speech and found herself hoping more than anything that Gabi would win first place at the Cheese Festival.

Gabi set the cheese and another slice of bread in front of Julia, motioning for her to take another serving.

"Has your nephew always lived with you?" Julia asked, worried that if she didn't distract her hostess with conversation, Gabi would keep feeding her.

"He is here only temporarily. His house is . . ." She looked toward the kitchen door and stood, motioning for Julia to accompany her. "Come see for yourself."

They stepped outside, staying on the gravel track that ran around the house and away from the muddy puddles. The rain had stopped, leaving the air fresh and the earth damp. It was still a bit chilly, especially with Julia's wet hair.

Surrounding the house, Gabi's garden was splendid. Wrought-iron café sets and stone benches were set beneath grand trees, and honey-colored paths lined with rows of lavender ran among beds of herbs, shaped shrubs, and colorful flowers.

Chickens wandered among the plants. A coop and what appeared to be a small livestock barn were fenced to one side. Julia could hear the bleating of goats from that direction.

"There." Gabi pointed past her garden and to the hills beyond. Olive trees, their silver leaves rippling in the breeze, covered the flat land and moved up the hills in one direction, and on the other side of a dirt track, the rows of grape vines stood straight like disciplined soldiers. "You can just see Luc's house at the very edge of the family property." Gabi pointed past the olive grove to a large stone structure with a horse paddock and a barn beside it. "Long ago, the building was used as a winery."

Even from here, Julia could see Monsieur Paquet's house was a shambles. Part of the roof was covered by canvas tarps, and scaffolding holding stones and buckets ran along one outer wall.

"The olives grow wild"—Gabi motioned to the hills rising at the edge of the property—"climbing up the hills and into the mountains. But here . . ." She pointed to the flat area between Luc's house and her own. "These olives here are cultivated. Luc grows cuttings in the nursery to transplant into the groves." She indicated another structure closer to the hills.

"And what is that?" Julia pointed to a stone building directly in the center of the vineyard and the groves. It was smaller than the other buildings, but it looked well maintained.

"In my father's time, that building was used for wine tasting. Customers would come, and he would treat them to samples. There is a cellar below. But now, it is for storage." She looked to her right at the vineyard. "Once, all of this belonged to the Paquet family, but much has changed."

Julia knew nothing about grapes, but she thought the vines looked small. Maybe their size was usual for spring.

"Out beyond the vineyard is a lily pond I quite enjoy. There is a lovely old stone bridge surrounded by lavender fields. In the spring the hills are covered with poppies. You should visit it while you are here. Perhaps Luc will take you."

"I would like that," Julia said. Her reply was automatic, as her thoughts turned over the bits of information Gabi had given. It appeared Luc's house was in disrepair, the winery was closed down, and Luc was being forced to sell off parts of his family land. Apparently, he struggled financially. She felt sorry for the man. Farming must be difficult, and if she remembered correctly, many, if not all, of the vineyards had suffered from a blight that had killed off their vines within the last few decades. Had it affected the Paquet family as well, then? She didn't think it polite to ask. But she wished to help the people who had so willingly rescued her in her time of need.

When they returned to the kitchen, Julia insisted Gabi allow her to wash the dishes. Gabi argued for a moment but in the end acquiesced, having mending to finish. She sat in the soft chair beside the hearth, humming as she stitched a torn seam.

Julia wondered briefly if the shirt Gabi was repairing belonged to her nephew. But all other thoughts went from her head as she surveyed the pile of dishes in the washbasin and stacked on the counter beside it, some which had apparently sat dirty for days. The task would not be a quick one.

"Very well," she muttered, pushing up the sleeves of her blouse. Julia rather enjoyed a challenge, and she found putting a disorganized mess to rights to be quite a satisfying endeavor.

She began by taking all of the dishes from the basin and filling it with water. Then she collected the dirty dishes, utensils, pots, and bowls from around the kitchen, and the few she'd seen on the table in the front hall, stacking them beside the sink and even on the floor once there was no more room on the counter.

She cleared a space on the table for the clean dishes and set to work.

An hour and a half later, Julia wiped the last spoon dry and set it on the table with the others. Seeing the piles of gleaming dishes was very gratifying, and she took a moment to admire her work. She considered the shelves on the wall and looked into the drawers on the hutch and realized the dishes didn't appear to belong in a specific place. Perhaps she simply didn't understand Gabi's organizational system.

"Gabi, how would you like me to put the dishes away?" Julia asked. "I'm not certain where things belong."

Gabi looked up from the sock she was stitching and shook her head. "Ah, ma chérie, it is rather overwhelming, oui? I inherited pots from my grandmother, dishes from my husband's mother, bowls and utensils from my sister . . ." She waved her hands as she spoke, giving a sigh. "All of it has all accumulated to the point where I cannot find what I need, and once I do, I don't know where to put it when I'm finished."

Julia looked around the kitchen, imagining where she might put things if it were her own. The room had plenty of storage. Shelves, drawers, and cupboards in the hutch. If there were less clutter, she thought Gabi would find her kitchen much more comfortable and use the space more efficiently.

"I could organize the kitchen if you'd like," Julia said. "It is something I'm particularly good at, and I would love to have a way to repay you for your hospitality."

"Oh, ma Juliette, the task—she is *énorme.*" Gabi clasped her hands and shook her head. "Surely you do not wish to undertake such a thing."

"I would do it happily," Julia said. "If you'll trust me with it."

"Oh, oui, I trust you." Gabi grimaced, but she looked as if she were considering the idea. "But I do not like to burden you with my mess."

"Et voilà. It is settled." Julia clapped her hands. "But before I begin, show me your favorite things. The bowls you use most often, your favorite decorative pottery, a pot with sentimental value—that sort of thing."

After a few moments of discussion, Gabi left to milk the goat and tend to the herbs in her garden, and Julia launched into action.

She emptied the drawers and cupboards, finding quite a mixture of treasures as she did so: a partially eaten package of chocolates, a crumpled dishrag, a wrench, a bit of molded cheese, and a thimble. She cleared off the shelves and counters and sorted everything on the table, folding the laundry and setting it on the chairs. Then, using hot water, she wiped out the cupboards and drawers and washed off every shelf.

Inside the pantry, she used a stool to reach the top shelves, discovering old cans and jars that had long been forgotten. She wiped off the shelves and arranged the bottles in neat rows, as well as the jars of spices. Finding a basket, she filled it with root vegetables and anything else that should remain cool and took it below to the cellar.

As she moved the dishes to their places, Julia paid close attention, ensuring that the things Gabi used the most were within easy reach. She put two extra colanders and a pile of mismatched plates, along with other duplicates, into a crate she found outside the kitchen door. Gabi owned enough ladles for an entire town. Anything that was broken went into the crate as well.

The shelves on either side of the window over the sink Julia saved for special trinkets and a few flowerpots, thinking Gabi would not only appreciate colorful blooms while she washed dishes but would find it easy to water them as well. She dusted a photograph, returning it to the mantel beside a vase, and stored kitchen linens in a cupboard beneath the hutch.

Not knowing what to do with the crate and the piles of laundry from the table, she moved them to the small parlor. She could put them away later, once she knew where Gabi wanted everything to go.

Julia glanced out the window and noticed the afternoon had grown late. She looked at her two timepieces and saw that she had been working steadily for more than four hours. Soon it would be time to prepare supper.

She took the vase Gabi had explained had been a wedding gift fifty years earlier and hurried out into the yard with a knife. She hoped Gabi would not be upset if she cut a few flowers and within a moment had a gorgeous arrangement of peonies, roses, and of course, lavender.

Julia had just set the vase in the center of the table and the knife in the sink when Gabi entered the kitchen.

She let out a gasp and put her hands over her mouth. "Oh, ma chérie Juliette! *C'est merveilleux!*" Spinning around, she took it all in. "Everything is so bright and open. I . . . cannot believe . . ."

"I put a crate of extra dishes in your parlor," Julia said, not wanting Gabi to think she'd thrown away her things.

"Oh, how I will love to cook in such a kitchen. It feels brand-new," Gabi said. She embraced Julia, giving her a kiss on each cheek. "How shall we celebrate? We shall have wine, of course." She started to the pantry.

Julia grinned, delighted by the woman's reaction. "Do you like gugelhupf cake?"

CHAPTER SIX

Julia woke, and she stretched beneath the purple sheets. The sunlight that filtered into the Lavender Room was faint, and through the sheer curtains, the sky bore a hint of pink. The morning was still early, and she heard no noise in the house. Julia was warm and comfortable in the bed. She rolled over and closed her eyes, but the prospect of the unknown day ahead wouldn't allow her to fall back asleep.

She felt well rested and very happy, and it took only a moment to think of why. She'd worked hard the day before, and her efforts had been met with thanks and praise. Knowing she'd found a way to help gave her a warm feeling, and she decided that since she was to spend three more days in Provence, she would find other ways to be helpful to her hosts.

She'd spent a lovely evening with Gabi, preparing dinner, eating, and then listening to the older woman's stories for hours next to the fire as she ran her fingers over Fredric's soft fur. Between the two, they'd eaten nearly all the cake, saving only one piece for Gabi's nephew.

M. Paquet hadn't returned before the women retired for the night. Gabi expressed concern a few times, telling Julia his extended absence was very unusual—he rarely missed dinner—but she'd consoled herself that her nephew was a grown man and able to take care of himself. Julia couldn't help but wonder what kind of errand kept a man away so late, but of course, it was none of her business.

Deciding that she'd lolled about long enough, Julia rose. She checked her wristwatch and the pocket watch she kept on a ribbon. The hour was past six. She pulled a shawl around her shoulders and stepped to the window, pushing aside the curtains.

When she did, something large and brown fell to the floor beside her feet and crawled toward her bare toes.

Though she had never actually seen one, she recognized the creature from drawings: pinchers, a long curved tail with a barb at the tip . . . a scorpion!

Julia screamed and jumped onto the bed. The scorpion must have come in through the window. Were there more? It changed direction, coming toward the bed, and she screamed again.

The door crashed open, and M. Paquet burst inside, fastening his trousers, his hair stuck up in all directions. His gaze moved quickly around the room.

"Oh, Monsieur Paquet! Thank goodness." Julia pointed to the ground next to the bed. "*Faites attention!*" She shouted the warning and gasped, her hands shaking.

M. Paquet snatched up one of Julia's borrowed shoes and smashed it down on the intruder just as Gabi hurried into the room wearing a very sheer nightdress and a cap over her hair.

"What has happened?" Gabi pressed a hand to her heart.

"A scorpion," Julia explained, averting her eyes from Gabi's ensemble. She pulled her shawl tighter, and feeling silly for standing on the bed, she knelt on the mattress, peering over the edge to where M. Paquet had crouched down to look underneath the shoe. "Are there more?"

"The lavender." Gabi stepped around Luc and waved at the windowsill. "Where is the lavender?"

Julia tipped her head, confused. "I don't . . ."

Gabi put her fists on her hips. "The smell—it repels *les scorpions.*"

"Oh, I didn't realize . . ." Julia winced, remembering how she'd thought the dried flowers were simply an indication of Gabi's negligence. "I brushed them into the bin."

Gabi shook her head, tsking while her nephew moved to look beneath the wardrobe. After a moment, he stood. "I think it was only the one."

"And where were you last night?" Gabi asked, turning to him. "You returned very late."

"I went to Monteaux to find Marcel Bernard before he left for the Wine Festival in Orange."

"Why would you go all the way to Monteaux just to speak to Marcel Bernard?" Gabi's lip curled.

Apparently, Marcel Bernard was not her favorite person.

"Orange has a telegraph office." M. Paquet tipped his head toward Julia. "I did not want Mademoiselle Weston's father to worry."

"I was worried, mon cher. I'm glad you are home safely." Gabi patted his arm. "And it was very thoughtful of you." She let out a heavy breath and picked up Fredric the cat as he came curiously into the room. "Oh la la. My heart." She turned Fredric around to speak directly to his furry face. "What a way to awaken!" Gabi set down the cat again and started from the room, calling back over her shoulder as she passed through the door. "Remember the lavender, Juliette."

"I will." Julia grimaced. "And I apologize for frightening you."

M. Paquet crouched down and wiped the scorpion's remains with a handkerchief.

"You sent a telegram to Paris?" Julia stood and folded her arms over the shawl. The cat weaved between her feet.

"Oui." He folded the handkerchief, holding it by its edges.

She considered what the telegram might have said. Knowing M. Paquet, his explanation for her failure to arrive in Paris would have been brief. Had he made her look incompetent? Her stomach felt tight at the thought of her father's disappointment. And how did M. Paquet know where to send it in the first place? "Why did you not tell me that's what you were doing?" she asked. "I would have instructed you on what to say and where to address it . . ."

His brow rose. "I directed it to Colonel Weston, *Commissaire Expert des Beaux-Arts*, British Exhibition Headquarters."

Julia crouched and scratched Fredric's head. She grudgingly admitted the telegram would have found her father. But what had it said? She couldn't shake the tight feeling in her chest. Had M. Paquet's telegram made her look foolish? Was her father right now thinking she should never travel, or do anything for that matter, alone?

She directed her frustrations at the man in front of her. "Orange has a telegraph office? Does it also have a train station? If I'd gone with you, I could have continued on to Orange with Monsieur Bernard and been in Paris by now."

M. Paquet's eyes narrowed. "Oui, I considered it. But I was faster alone. I knew Marcel would leave well before dark. I only just caught him as it was."

"Well, I do wish you'd told me," Julia said, standing straight and folding her arms. "Especially as your errand pertained to me directly."

M. Paquet opened his mouth as if he'd say something further but closed it again. He frowned and left the Lavender Room, closing the door behind him.

Julia felt a pinch of guilt. She'd been unkind, finding fault when she should have been offering thanks for the effort he'd made in her behalf, not to mention his saving her from the scorpion. But his acting without consulting her was just like her father's hiring a chaperone when one wasn't necessary. Why did neither of them consider her input on matters directly affecting her own life? Why did nobody trust her judgment?

Once Julia made up the bed, Fredric made himself at home among the pillows. Julia continued to fret as she dressed, tying the borrowed apron and arranging the scarf over her hair. She took her time, straightening the room, not wishing to meet M. Paquet on the stairs—or worse, in the washroom.

Finally, hearing his footsteps descend the stairs, she waited a moment longer, then opened her door. The smell of breakfast filled the house, and Julia wished she'd hurried down to help Gabi with the meal instead of hiding away in her room. Today it felt as if she couldn't do anything right. She stepped down the stairs but paused in the entry hall beside the painting of Gabi's house as she heard M. Paquet's voice in the kitchen. He did not sound happy at all.

"I always keep my cup right here, on this shelf by the sink," he said.

"Well, now it is put away properly," Gabi said.

"And what happened to everything?" M. Paquet continued. "Where is the sugar?"

"In the pantry, where it belongs. Juliette has arranged it all; isn't that wonderful?"

M. Paquet grumbled something Julia couldn't hear. She assumed it was because he had moved into the pantry. And from the tone of his voice, she didn't think what he had to say was exactly charitable with regards to her or to the tidied kitchen.

"I do hope the olive seedlings survived their journey from Athens," Gabi said.

"An extra day inside the crate didn't help," Luc said. "They are already delicate. I should have planted them immediately upon my return."

"But you did a very good thing, riding all the way to Monteaux. A father's mind is at ease, and that is worth more than the few shoots you might have lost."

M. Paquet grumbled something else.

Julia's pinch of guilt tightened.

"I can help plant," Gabi offered. "The chore will go faster with two."

"You've your own work to do this morning," he said. "Coquette will miss you, and your garden will as well. I'll manage in the nursery."

"Mon cher, you seem unhappy today." Gabi's voice was concerned.

"I'm happy," Luc said. "Just a little tired from all the travel."

"Ah yes. Few things are as uncomfortable as a long horse ride. The stiffness in your back and the chafing in your—"

"I'll see you at lunch, Gabi," M. Paquet interrupted, sounding as if he were holding back a laugh.

Julia heard the kitchen door open and close.

"Childbirth's no holiday either," Gabi muttered. "Or arthritis." She turned away from the door and smiled when Julia entered. "Ah, Juliette. I didn't wish you a proper good morning." She kissed both of Julia's cheeks. "It's a lovely day today, non? And my kitchen is so orderly. It puts me in high spirits."

"I'm glad to hear it," Julia said. She sat in the chair Gabi motioned her to and took a slice of bread. "I didn't mean to eavesdrop, but I overheard you mention that M. Paquet was unable to take care of his seedlings yesterday."

"Eh, oui. They should be planted as soon as possible. And I know he hopes to graft the new buds now, when the weather is still cool. Farmers— always they must depend on the weather. And with last year's drought and the years before with the blight on the vines . . . Provence, she has not been kind to those who depend on her for their living."

Gabi spoke with a smile, but Julia could see sadness in her eyes. And worry. "Do you think . . . should I help him plant today?"

"Oh, I think he would love that, ma chérie."

The two finished breakfast, and Gabi left to tend to her goat and garden. Julia remained to clean the dishes. While she worked, the tight feeling remained in her stomach. She must apologize to M. Paquet for her discourteous words this morning and thank him for his kindness. Helping plant the seedlings might just be the way to clear the air between them.

The sounds of Gabi yelling startled her, and Julia almost dropped the plate she was drying. She set it down and rushed outside to see what was wrong.

She found Gabi pulling a rope with a protesting goat at the other end toward a short, squat woman on the far side of her property. Julia wasn't certain whether Gabi was yelling at the woman or the goat, and as she got closer, she realized it was both.

". . . again in my garden," Gabi was saying. "I shall have no mint left, and she trampled down an entire row of rosemary."

"Fleur is a clever goat," the woman replied, arms folded. "She can escape her pen as well as give the sweetest milk."

"It is my garden that makes the winning chèvre so sweet," Gabi said. "Yet you take home the prize every year."

"Jealousy does not look good on you, Gabrielle." The woman folded her arms.

"A stained apron does not look good on you, Alice, but I am too polite to mention it." Gabi glared at her.

Alice looked down at her apron, which was indeed stained, and frowned at Gabi. When she saw Julia approach, she raised a brow and looked back at Gabi with a questioning expression.

"Alice, this is my guest, Juliette Weston from Paris."

"A guest?" Alice said. "When have you ever had a guest? And how do you know someone from Paris?" She looked Julia up and down. "She doesn't dress like she's from Paris."

Gabi ignored the woman's commentary. "Juliette, this is Alice Laurent, my neighbor." She spoke the last two words with a sigh, as if having a neighbor were a burden she endured stoically. She motioned with her chin toward the house close to hers.

"Bonjour, Madame Laurent," Julia said.

Alice continued to study her. "Is she Luc's friend? I'll wager she is Luc's friend. It's about time he brought a young lady around." She spoke as if Julia were not present or as though she could not hear. And since the woman's questions apparently didn't require answers, Julia didn't offer any.

A man's voice called out a greeting, and the three women looked toward the Laurents' house.

"Mathieu Laurent," Gabi told Julia as the man approached. "Alice's husband."

The man was short and wide like his wife. He walked toward them slowly, limping as he leaned on a cane. A little dog followed at his heels. "How pleasant to look through my window this morning and see three beautiful women." In spite of how painful his movements appeared, he spoke with twinkling eyes.

Alice huffed through her nose.

"Good morning, Mathieu," Gabi said. "This is my dear friend Juliette Weston."

"A tremendous pleasure, mademoiselle." Monsieur Laurent swept up Julia's hand and kissed it. "We receive few visitors here in Riv, and each one is a gift."

Alice rolled her eyes and let out another huff.

"*Un plaisir*, Monsieur Laurent," Julia said, remembering she'd seen his name at the train station. "You are the stationmaster?"

"Eh, oui." He shrugged.

From his tone, Julia didn't think he took his position very seriously.

"I found Fleur in my garden again." Gabi pulled on the rope, tugging the dark-brown goat away from the patch of grass the animal was eating.

"*Encore?*" Mathieu groaned, shaking his head. "This goat! She is such trouble. She has learned to unknot her rope."

"We cannot blame the goat for being too clever to remain in her pen, Mathieu," Alice said. She took the rope from Gabi and scratched Fleur beneath her chin.

"We *can* blame her for ruining my garden," Gabi retorted. "My Coquette, she is so well-behaved." Gabi pointed toward her own goat pen, where a light-brown goat with white spots munched on a wad of something.

"Your garden will recover," Alice replied. "It always does. And if anyone is to complain, it is myself. I know my hens have been laying in your garden, and you've kept the eggs."

"If the eggs are in my garden, they are my eggs," Gabi said. "How am I to know which chicken laid which? Ask them?"

"My hens lay pink-colored eggs, and yours do not. Perhaps you need spectacles."

"Perhaps you need to learn to manage your animals."

The women's argument escalated, their voices speaking over one another until Julia couldn't hear anything besides angry yelling.

Mathieu shook his head. "They will go on like this all day," he muttered in a low voice.

Julia smiled. She patted his dog on the head. "Perhaps I should go. I planned to help M. Paquet in the nursery today."

"You should make your escape now, or you'll be drawn into it." He widened his eyes, giving a warning, but his expression held a tease.

"*Excuse moi*, Monsieur Laurent," Julia whispered.

He tugged on his soft hat's brim and winked.

Julia followed his advice and hurried away, hearing the ladies' arguing behind her the entire way through the garden and down the path to the nursery.

CHAPTER SEVEN

Julia hesitated outside the nursery. She studied the building for a moment. It was constructed of the same peach-and-gray rock as the other structures on the property and had a tile roof. Stacks of pots were piled around the walls, and heavy wooden shutters hung at the windows. Instead of sky blue like the shutters at Gabi's house, the wood appeared to have been painted red at one time, but most of the paint had peeled away.

She stepped onto the threshold. Should she knock? Call out? Enter? In the end, she did all three. She knocked and pushed the door open. "Monsieur Paquet, are you here?" she called as she stepped inside.

She saw him right away and felt foolish for using such a loud voice in the small building. M. Paquet was in the center of the crowded room, holding a shovel. When she entered, he glanced toward the door, then returned to his work.

The smell of damp earth was nearly overwhelming. Julia stepped through the space, careful to avoid trays, buckets, and pots of various sizes holding dirt and plants. Garden tools and more pots were on the worktables along both sides of the room, and still more were beneath. Pots were stacked chaotically in the corners, and here and there, a larger container held a bush or a small tree. She stepped around the two crates from the train and avoided shards of broken pottery and branches sticking out of a bucket of water. It appeared the man had inherited his aunt's organization skills.

M. Paquet was shoveling dirt and what appeared to be . . . different dirt . . . into a wide barrel and stirring to blend them together. He didn't glance up, even when Julia stood directly in front of him.

She grimaced. He was obviously still bothered by her dismissive reaction earlier. "Bonjour, M. Paquet," she said in a careful voice.

He grunted and scooped another shovelful, pouring it into the bucket.

Julia stepped back to keep a spill of dirt from landing on her shoes. "Monsieur, I thought perhaps I might help you this morning. I know your seedlings need to be planted quickly, and riding to Monteaux has already put you a day behind schedule."

M. Paquet straightened. He rested his arm on the shovel handle and his gaze on her, one brow raised.

He may need more convincing. "Monsieur, I would like to apologize. I neglected to thank you for what you did. I did not mean to react so poorly. I was rather flustered when I found the scorpion and worried about—" She stopped, not wishing to get into the details of her relationship with her father. "Anyway, I am sorry. And I thank you for what you did." She picked up a pair of dirty gloves from a worktable and pushed her hands inside, brushing them together. "Now, where would you like me to start?"

M. Paquet studied her for a moment, then pushed the shovel deep into the barrel, leaving it there and motioning with a tip of his head. "*Venez ici.*"

He stepped past her and pulled open one of the crate lids, then crouched down and reached inside.

Julia crouched beside him.

He lifted out a small plant about six inches long with a piece of cloth tied around its roots and inspected it for a moment before handing it to her.

Julia took it, cradling the ball of roots carefully in her palm as he had. She recognized the slender olive leaves.

"These are the new seedlings, as you can see," he said. "Fifty of them." He lifted off the other crate's lid, revealing the rest of the bundled plants. He reached inside and took out a pouch. "And here are the new seeds."

"And they all must be planted?" Julia asked.

"Most of the cuttings will be grafted onto the existing trees." He pointed to the bucketful of branches. "And I must do that today or tomorrow, at the very latest. But the others, oui. They need planting."

"Very well." Julia rose, holding the seedling gently. "Show me what to do."

"I'm preparing the soil for the seedlings now." He led her back to the barrel of dirt with the shovel. "They will be planted in those pots." He motioned to a haphazard pile of small containers in one corner of the room.

Julia set the seedling on an empty spot on a worktable and picked up one of the pots, then brought it back to where he had gone back to mixing the soil. "There is some dirt in here; should I dump it out? Or put the fresh soil in with it?"

"Dump it," he said. He pointed to another bucket.

She found a small shovel on the worktable. She poured out the old dirt and scooped new soil into the pot, noticing that it was very fine, like sand. Once the pot was filled, she set it on the worktable.

M. Paquet came to stand next to her. He showed her how to hollow out a spot for the new plant with her fingers, then to remove the cloth wrapping from the roots of the seedling. "*Attentivement*," he warned. "Disturb the roots as little as possible."

Julia set the seedling gently into the little hollow, glancing up at her companion to make certain she was doing it correctly.

He nodded and pressed the soil around the roots. "Et voilà. She is planted."

Julia smiled. The task was simple and surprisingly satisfying. She admired the little seedling in its pot. "How long before it grows into a tree?"

"A few years," he said. He pointed to one of the larger trees in the nursery. "This one was planted two years ago. It will be ready to go into the ground this spring—once the nights are warmer."

"I see," Julia said.

"It will be at least five years before it bears any fruit."

"Such a long time." She was surprised. "It must be frustrating to wait."

He motioned toward the branches in the bucket of water. "The cuttings will grow faster, grafted into the existing trees. Some should bear fruit as soon as next year."

"Why do you not use cuttings exclusively?" she asked. "What is the advantage of seeds and seedlings when they take so long to grow?"

"There are a few reasons." He picked up the little pot with the seedling inside. "This variety was chosen because of its fruit. It is especially favorable for oil. Others produce olives better suited for pickling." He set the pot back on the table. "Some of my family's trees are hundreds of years old. Their roots are strong enough to withstand the Mistral winds, and they will survive extreme temperatures. But disease has killed some of the branches; others have simply stopped producing fruit. If the roots are strong and the tree is healthy, new buds can be grafted into the bark, and the tree will bear fruit once again." He brought another seedling from the crate to the table. "An olive tree grows slowly, but it will last for generations. So what we do today is not just for now but for . . ." He motioned with his hand.

"For your grandchildren," Julia finished.

"Oui. Things of great value—they take time to build." He smiled softly. "*Mon père* used to say that." He looked toward the window. "These trees, this grove, it is more than just a farm. It is my family's legacy."

Julia wondered whether he carried on out of duty or whether he enjoyed the work. He certainly felt strongly about it. As she listened to him, she considered that she had not been entirely fair in her judgment of Monsieur Paquet. He was curt at times and rather sloppy, but hearing him talk about his family's work, seeing the intensity in his expression . . . a wiggle moved through her middle, and heat rose to her cheeks. She realized the man stood very close.

She pushed the newly potted plant away from the edge of the table and got a new pot from the corner. This one didn't have dirt in it, but there was a spiderweb inside. She shivered, remembering the scorpion, and felt grateful for the thick gloves.

Monsieur Paquet set the pot with the seedling back on the table and returned to the task of mixing the soil.

Julia scooped soil into the pot, prepared it, and planted the next seedling, setting it beside the first. The worktable was already crowded with tools and twine and more containers, and she knew fifty small pots would not fit in the space. "Might I move these to make room for the others?" She waved her hand toward the cluttered table.

"Oui."

She was glad for a project to focus her thoughts and calm the strange emotions that had arisen so suddenly from . . . somewhere. Having things in order was just what she needed. She removed the empty containers from the table and stacked them with the others. Then she moved the pots holding plants to the back of the table, against the wall. She transferred the tools to the other worktable. Finding a cloth, she wiped away dirt until she had a clean workspace, then began emptying out the little pots, pouring out the old dry dirt and wiping away spiderwebs. She stacked the pots neatly in rows on the table. When she glanced up at M. Paquet, she saw he was watching her with an amused expression.

She felt immediately defensive. "Do you find something diverting, monsieur?"

"I have never met such a tidy woman." His tone was not mocking but friendly.

Julia relaxed and shrugged. "I like things to be organized. Then I can complete the task in the most efficient manner."

The corners of his lips twitched. "I see."

"You *will* see, Monsieur Paquet." She held up a finger to emphasize the point. "I will finish planting in no time because I made the extra effort to set things in order at the start."

His lips twitched again. "Luc," he said. "You should call me Luc."

Heat returned to her cheeks, and she looked down at the little seedlings, moving the pots. "I don't think that would be appropriate, monsieur."

"This isn't Paris. Here, in Provence, we speak much less formally."

"Oh." Julia didn't know what to say. A man had never asked her to call him by his forename.

"Besides, you and I—we sleep across the corridor from one another, like a brother and sister. It is silly to stand on ceremony with such an arrangement, non?"

He took the twine and a knife from the table and then moved toward the door, picking up the bucket of cuttings and the wide brimmed hat leaning against it. "I will fetch you for lunch, Juliette?"

"Yes." She wiped imaginary dirt from the table with the cloth, needing to keep her hands busy and to look at something besides him. "Thank you."

Once the door closed, Julia stopped wiping the table. "Luc," she said softly, enjoying how it sounded. And surprisingly, she'd enjoyed how her name sounded when he'd said it as well. But she did not at all enjoy his suggestion that the two were like brother and sister.

Feeling the anticipation of a project, Julia set to work. She dragged the crates of seedlings closer to the worktable and tried to move the barrel, but it was too heavy. No matter. Within a moment, she had developed a system: take a pot to the barrel, and once it was filled with soil, bring it with a new seedling back to the table to plant. The work moved quickly, and at last, she planted the final seedling.

Seeing the pots lined up with their little sprouts all tidily planted gave her the pleasant, satisfied feeling that always accompanied the completion of a task.

Julia looked at her wristwatch and the watch hanging from her neck. Having still a few hours until lunchtime, she decided the rest of the nursery could use straightening as well.

She set the pouch of olive seeds on the worktable and moved the empty crates outside the door. She found an old broom and pulled out the pots from beneath the tables so she could sweep behind them. She cleaned off the other worktable, swept out the cobwebs and piles of spilled dirt from the corners of the room, and then cleaned out the old pots, dumping the old dirt into the bucket. She brought the pots in from outside the building and stacked all of the empty pots neatly under the tables. Some of the containers beneath the table had plants in them, and these she moved to the top, where they could get the sunlight they needed.

She pushed and pulled the heavier pots of trees on the ground to the far wall, arranging them by size.

Seeing nails in the wall, Julia hung as many tools up and out of the way as she could, and the rest she put into buckets or leaned nicely in a corner.

Luc still hadn't come for her, and she decided planting the olive seeds was an easy enough task. She'd planted bean seeds in school, and it was much simpler than the seedlings had been. She opened the pouch and poured out the seeds, then found small pots for them, filled them with soil, pressed the seeds in, and covered them.

Finally, she took the watering can out to the pump in the garden and filled it, making the trip back and forth a few times until everything was watered thoroughly.

The nursery looked splendid, and Julia could not stop her smile when she thought of how pleased Luc would be when he saw it.

When Luc returned a quarter of an hour later, Julia stood back to allow him to see the space in its entirety. He took a few steps inside and turned slowly, taking it all in. He was apparently too delighted to speak.

"Juliette . . ."

"It was really no trouble," she said. She clasped her hands in front of her waist. His reaction was even better than she'd imagined. He was actually speechless. A warm bubble expanded in her chest.

He set down the bucket with the remainder of the cuttings by the door. He looked at Julia, then at the nursery. "It is very tidy."

"Much better, don't you agree?" Julia fought against her grin. She felt very proud to have done such a splendid job in such a short amount of time.

Luc scratched his jaw, his gaze moving over the room as if searching for the right words to express his pleasure at the surprise. "You finished the planting, I see." He walked between the tables, looking at all of the pots. He picked up one of the newly planted seedlings. A trickle of water drained out of the hole in the bottom of the pot, and Luc winced.

A tinge of unease began inside her. "Is something . . . did I do something wrong?"

Luc lifted another little pot, letting it drip. "The cuttings are very delicate at this stage," he said. "They need to remain dry."

"Oh."

"And out of the sun."

Her stomach got hot. "I assumed all plants need water and sunlight."

He didn't respond but lifted a few other pots, watching the water drain out. "Juliette." Luc lifted the seed pouch. His voice was calm, but she could tell he exerted an effort to keep it so. "Where are the olive seeds?"

"I planted them," she said in a quiet voice, praying it hadn't been the wrong thing to do as well. She joined him at the table. "They are in these pots, here."

Luc nodded, and his lips pressed together.

"That was wrong as well, wasn't it?" Julia asked.

"The seeds need to be prepared first." He pulled off his hat and rubbed the back of his neck. "And these"—he indicated the pots she'd moved to the sides of the room—"they were arranged by variety and age. I—"

"I'm sorry." A sick feeling compressed her stomach. "I thought . . ." Her throat got tight, and she blinked at the stinging in her eyes. Instead of putting the nursery in order, she'd made everything worse. She hurried over and started to drag one of the heavy pots back toward the center of the room. "I will put them all back. And dig out the seeds. And put the seedlings in dry soil."

Luc muttered something she couldn't hear. He rubbed his forehead and sighed, looking around the room. "It can all be put right after lunch. Come along. Gabi is waiting." He moved to the door and held it open, gesturing for her to precede him.

Julia glanced at him as they walked along the path through Gabi's garden. His mouth was pulled tight, and the lines between his brows were deep. She felt utterly deflated and rather ill. "Luc, I am so sorry. I thought I was being helpful."

He glanced at her. "I know." His face softened slightly. "And I'm thankful for the effort. The nursery has never been so orderly."

"But I ruined everything." She hung her head. "And I made more work." A new thought jolted her. "Will the seedlings survive?" The idea of him losing the seedlings he'd brought all the way from Greece made her stomach drop.

"I think so." He nodded. "After lunch, I'll replant them in dry soil, and they'll go beneath the table, out of the sunlight."

"I will help you set it all right," she said, determined to fix what she'd done." With the two of us working together, it will—"

"Perhaps Gabi could use your help in the house this afternoon." Luc opened the door to Gabi's kitchen.

His voice was not angry, but there was no mistaking his intention. He'd had quite enough of her assistance.

Julia's chest burned, and she swallowed against the lump in her throat. She moved past Luc into the house, not daring to look up at his face, lest she start to cry. She'd started out this morning hoping to make things better with Luc, but she'd managed to do the exact opposite.

CHAPTER EIGHT

JULIA DID NOT ADD MUCH to the conversation at lunch; instead, she fed bits of her food to Fredric and his black-and-white sister. She felt terrible for the trouble she'd caused Luc. And the more she considered, the more ashamed she was. What arrogance to believe she knew better than he how to manage his business.

"Juliette, you have hardly touched your *andouillette*," Gabi said. "Are you ill, ma chérie?"

Julia forced a smile. "No, not at all." She took a bite of the sausage and commented on how delicious the food tasted.

"You must keep up your strength," Gabi said. "Working in the nursery can be very tiring."

Julia broke off a piece of bread and spread the chèvre cheese over it. She kept her gaze from Luc, feeling a thickness in the air between them.

"And how did you get on?" Gabi asked, cutting into her sausage. "Did you manage to get all of the seedlings planted?"

"Oui," Luc said.

Julia hazarded a peek at him, but he didn't look up from his plate.

Gabi looked between them, her gaze turning thoughtful, but she did not comment further. Instead, she filled Luc in on the morning's confrontation with the Laurents about Fleur the goat. "And does she just expect me to allow her animal to eat my garden?" Gabi finished the story with a huff.

"Maybe I will have a look at the Laurents' pen," Luc said. "Figure out how Fleur keeps getting out."

"I'm sure Mathieu would appreciate it," Gabi agreed. "He tries to manage all the chores as he used to, but it is so much more difficult lately with his hip . . ."

Luc grunted in agreement. He pushed back from the table and stood. "Thank you for lunch, Gabi."

"I will see you at suppertime." Gabi let him kiss her cheek. "And Juliette, will you return to the nursery with Luc?"

Julia looked up, meeting Luc's gaze and feeling her face go crimson. The sick feeling returned. "I . . . no. Can I be of any use to you inside, Gabi?"

Luc left, and Gabi leaned forward, resting her arms on the table. "Ma chérie Juliette, tell me, what has happened?"

The heat returned to Julia's chest as she explained what she had done in the nursery that morning. "Luc didn't get angry, but I know he felt frustrated," she said.

Gabi swatted her hand through the air. "Don't worry about Luc. He's grateful for the help. And the nursery needed a good cleaning."

"I shouldn't have assumed my way was best," Julia said, looking down at the cat on her lap. She hated the thought of Luc out in the nursery right now, remembering with every seedling he replanted what a frustration she'd proven to be.

Gabi stood, taking their plates to the washbasin. "After we wash the dishes and prepare for dinner, I have a closet I'd planned to clean out. Do you know of anyone who might be able to help?" She winked and grinned.

"I might know someone." Julia smiled. She appreciated the attempt to cheer her up, and truthfully, the idea of a new project—one she couldn't bungle—did sound like just the thing.

Later that afternoon, Julia glanced at both of her timepieces. She and Gabi had worked steadily for more than three hours. Once they'd washed the dishes, set the bread rising, and cut up vegetables for a stew, the pair had cleaned out two closets, one wardrobe, and the curio cabinet in the parlor.

Gabi left to tend to Coquette, and Julia let out a heavy sigh as she sat on the parlor sofa, feeling exhausted from all the work.

Four crates sat on the parlor floor, filled with an assemblage of old clothing, kitchen implements, books, linen, and other odds and ends that had gathered in the nooks of Gabi's house over the years.

Julia was tempted to take a nap but decided the task wasn't completely finished until the crates were moved into storage. And wouldn't her hostess be pleased to return to find her parlor floor clean?

She hefted one of the crates and took it outside, starting down the garden path. Although the crate was heavy, Julia didn't stop to rest, wanting to get past the nursery as quickly as possible. Luckily, she did not encounter Luc, and she did not see him among the olive trees as she walked by either.

The storage building was unlocked. Julia held on to the heavy crate with both hands and pushed the door open with her hip.

She stopped in the doorway, blinking as she took in the sight before her. Where she'd imagined a dusty building filled with old furniture and boxes, she found instead a bright room with high windows. Paintings surrounded the space, some on easels, others propped up on boxes, and some were set on the floor, leaning against the walls.

A drop cloth was laid on the ground in a sunny spot in the center of the room, and on it was a table of supplies and an easel that held a canvas with a partially completed composition. Julia set down the crate and walked closer, studying the painting.

The paint colors were pastel, but their application wasn't delicate. The strokes were applied thickly, with subtly varying tones. She could see the painting was of a landscape, though the trees and other flora had only been sketched in with a pencil. A brook crossed through the field, and even in the early stages of the work, the water appeared to trickle and move over stones.

The way the artist captured movement and light—it must be the same person who'd painted the picture in Gabi's front entry. Julia stared at the painting, trying to imagine the person who'd created it.

"It's spectacular," Julia muttered. Was Gabi an artist? It stood to reason. She was creative, she surrounded herself with color, and as was the case with many artists Julia had met, she was a bit unconventional.

Papers with sketches and notes were scattered over the table with tubes of paint and cups filled with brushes. A stool with a paint-splattered apron was beside it. Julia examined the sketches for a moment. *Why did Gabi not tell me about this?* she wondered. She could not imagine the older woman being shy about anything.

Julia walked around the edges of the room, studying the works. The paintings had obviously been completed over a number of years. She recognized what must be some of the early attempts and marveled at the artist's improvement in others. When she reached a particular painting that sat up higher, on an easel, she stopped, drawing in a breath.

This one. This one is the masterpiece. The composition was different from that of the others. A woman was shown, leaning over a stone bridge, her arm outstretched toward a pair of swans she appeared to be feeding. The shadows of a willow played over the skin of the woman's shoulders and face, and the reflection of the light on the water shone on her as well, the contrast bringing movement to the picture.

Julia could not take her eyes from the woman's face. The artist had created the painting in the impressionist style, giving the feeling of a stolen moment or the wisp of a memory. The image was stunning—breathtaking—pulling at something deep inside Julia's heart and filling her with a longing that brought tears to her eyes.

"Juliette?" Luc's voice startled her, breaking the spell.

She turned quickly. "Oh, Luc." His expression was not pleased. Probably because he'd spent the afternoon replanting and reorganizing his nursery.

"What are you doing here?" he asked.

"I thought this building was for storage." Julia pointed to the crate by the door. "I didn't realize . . ." She cleared her throat, trying to expel the rush of emotion evoked by the painting. "Is this Gabi's studio?"

His expression grew, if possible, even darker beneath the shadow of his hat brim. "You should not trespass where you're not invited."

"But Gabi would not mind," Julia said. "I'm sure of it." She didn't like the way he made her feel as if she were doing something wrong. "I should like her to tell me about her work. And my father would be so pleased to discover an unknown artist, especially one with such talent." She motioned around the room. "All of this—it belongs in a gallery."

"It is *my* studio." He spoke in a low voice, the edges of his eyes tightening as if he'd not wanted to make the confession.

Julia gave a small gasp. "*You* are the artist." She looked around the room, viewing the artwork again with an entirely different perspective. Luc had created this? "But why did you not tell me when I asked about the painting in Gabi's front hall? That is obviously your work as well."

Luc shrugged. "I don't tell anyone." He pushed his hands into his pockets.

Julia couldn't believe it. She swept her arms wide. "You painted all of these?"

"Oui."

"They are . . . *you* are . . ." She motioned, unable to come up with words to describe exactly how splendid the works were. "You must have been trained."

"For a time." Luc moved to the easel, lifting the apron and sitting on the bench. He set his hat on the table. "I attended l'École des Beaux-Arts in Arles, but . . ." He shrugged again. "But I had to cut my studies short. When my parents died, I returned to Riv."

"To care for the trees," Julia finished.

"Oui. And for Gabi, although you should not tell her that. She does not believe she needs any help." He shuffled around some papers on the table, seeming to not wish to continue the discussion.

But he did not appear to mind her presence, so Julia continued around the room, considering each of the paintings. The more she saw, the more convinced she was that his artwork did not deserve to be hidden away in a shed in the country. He had as much, if not more skill than any impressionist artist she'd seen. And she had seen quite a few. For all of his potential to be wasted . . . Julia could not allow that to happen.

She returned to study the painting of the woman, feeling the same pull in her heart as before. "Luc, these paintings—*this* painting. It should be seen, not hidden away. Your name should be known and your work shown in a museum or a gallery's collection. You are a master."

Luc frowned, tossing his papers onto the table. "I am an olive farmer with a hobby."

"You could be more. I'm not simply giving polite praise. I know art. I've been exposed to it my entire life with my father. This . . ." She lifted her hand toward the painting of the woman. "It belongs in the l'Exposition Universelle."

"Non," Luc said.

"My father would—"

"Non, Juliette."

His voice was not angry, but he spoke firmly, leaving no room for argument. She turned back to the painting. Luc was wrong. This was not merely a hobby. A hobby created pleasant paintings of flowers and baskets of fruit. But this painting felt alive. This kind of work took something more than simply the ability to paint a recognizable image with pretty colors. The ability to reach deep inside one's heart and create something that spoke to another's soul . . . that was rare. A gift that came to few and was developed over years of study and practice. Luc was more than he was willing to admit. Was he afraid? Had his work been rejected before? She didn't think now was the time to ask. She'd upset him enough for one day.

Hearing scratching sounds behind her, she glanced back.

Luc had put on the apron, and he was mixing paint on a board. He dabbed in his brush and, tipping his head to the side, touched the paint to his canvas. That strange wiggling feeling moved through Julia's middle again as she watched him, and she felt the blush return to her cheeks.

"Who is she?" she asked.

Luc didn't glance up to see who she meant. "*Ma mère.*"

"She's beautiful." Julia turned back to the painting again, feeling as if she could happily look at it for hours. The feelings it drew from her were such a mixture of love and sadness that she couldn't help but want to know more. "How did she die?"

"Fever," he said. "And mon père five days later."

"While you were away at art school." She glanced back at him.

He nodded, his eyes not leaving the canvas.

"I'm sorry." She looked back at the painting and allowed her emotions to get pulled to the surface again. "Ma mère died in a carriage accident when I was three years old." The longing and sadness and love she felt when looking at Luc's painting filled her heart at the thought of her own mother. Julia hardly remembered her, just bits of memories, images that slipped away when she tried to see them clearly.

"I am sorry, Juliette."

She startled at the sound of his voice so close.

Luc stood beside her. He held out a handkerchief.

Julia took it, realizing there were tears on her cheeks. She had not cried for her mother in years.

"Oh, excuse-moi." She dabbed the handkerchief on her cheeks. "The painting . . ."

Luc glanced at it.

"It has a rather strong effect on me," she explained.

"Mothers . . . they are *extraordinaire*, non?" Luc said.

"Oui." Julia nodded. "But it is the artist who can stir up such emotions— *he* is *extraordinaire*." She handed back the handkerchief, feeling foolish for the personal nature of her compliment and for the display of emotion. She started for the exit. "I will see you at dinner, Luc."

Closing the door behind her, Julia let out a sigh. The last thing she'd intended when she'd taken a crate to the storage shed was to break down in tears. But, on the other hand, she hadn't intended to stumble upon Luc Paquet's secret art studio, either. The encounter left her with quite a lot to consider.

Why did Luc keep his art hidden? Was he simply a private person, or was it a matter of self-doubt? She was certain his works would be praised in the art community. The sale of any of his paintings would be enough to finish the repairs on his house. He could purchase back the grape vineyard and expand the farm. Or hire someone else to do the farm chores and have his days free to focus on his art.

She sighed, picking a sprig of lavender. Remembering the scorpion, she picked a handful and sniffed it as she walked. If Luc would only trust himself— and trust Julia. She may not know how much water to give an olive seedling, but in this, she was right.

She walked slowly up the garden path, enjoying the aroma of the lavender and the warm sun. Gabi's garden was truly a work of art. Perhaps Provence was not as utterly devoid of culture as she'd assumed.

A rustling sound from the other side of the garden caught her attention. "Oh no! Fleur." The dark goat was stepping through Gabi's herbs.

Julia looked around, hoping to see Gabi or one of the Laurents nearby to help, but no one was in sight. Only the two cats watched her from their perch on the garden wall. "Go on, Fleur. Shoo." She waved her hands, but the goat looked at her and kept chewing.

Julia glanced back at the storage building. She was not going to interrupt Luc again. She'd disturbed him enough for one day. She pushed the lavender into her apron pocket and clapped her hands together loudly. "Fleur, *allez-vous en!* Get out of the garden." But the noise didn't seem to bother the goat either.

Julia moved closer. The goat was larger than it had seemed when Gabi had been pulling on its rope. And it had two little horns. Would it charge at her? Did goats bite?

"You're a nice goat, aren't you, Fleur?" She crouched down slowly, picking up the lead rope. "Now, come along." She gave the rope a little tug.

Fleur didn't budge.

Julia tugged harder, and the goat took a step forward. "There you go." She hoped she didn't hurt the animal, pulling on the rope as she did. But Fleur seemed not to mind. "Let's get you back to the Laurents'," she said in as pleasant a voice as she could manage.

Not wanting to turn her back on the animal and give her the chance to charge at Julia or bite her heels, Julia walked backward through the garden, speaking in a soft voice as she pulled the rope. The goat didn't protest, but she didn't make the task easy, either. Fleur walked slowly and stopped every few steps to munch on some other plant in the garden. "That's it, time to go home. Gabi does not like it when you eat her herbs. You should know better."

When Julia reached the fence between the two properties, she stopped, not sure what to do with Fleur. Should she take the animal to the Laurents' front door or leave her at the fence where they would find her? Julia knew the goat could untie a knot, so she didn't think tying Fleur to the fence would work. She would just get back into the garden.

Julia looked around for a moment, wishing for a solution to materialize. If the Laurents were like Gabi, they would milk the goat in the evening—so Alice should come out at any time, looking for Fleur.

Julia spotted a tree, well away from Gabi's garden but near the Laurents' fence. It had a low enough branch that Julia could easily tie the goat's rope to it, but the goat couldn't reach to chew on the knot. And there were plenty of weeds and nonflowering bushes under the tree for Fleur to eat while she waited. It was the perfect solution.

Julia pulled the goat to the tree. "Here you go, Fleur. Now, stay here and wait for Alice." She tied the rope tightly to the branch and then reached out with a tentative hand to pat the goat on its neck. "Good girl."

The purr of a tabby cat and the smell of baking bread greeted her when she entered Gabi's kitchen. Julia had so many questions for Gabi. She wanted to know everything about Luc's art. Why didn't he tell anyone about his talent? Why was his art hidden away in a storage shed? But when she came inside, a wave of exhaustion hit, and she decided to ask her questions later, when she'd had time to consider exactly the words to use. She didn't want to offend or to sound nosy.

Julia listened to Gabi chatter as they finished preparing supper and put a cake into the oven, but her thoughts kept going back to the events of the day, especially those events that involved Luc.

CHAPTER NINE

AFTER DINNER, JULIA HELPED CLEAN and put away the dishes but excused herself before dessert and Gabi's proposed card game. While she did enjoy cards, she didn't imagine she would make very good company. Her arms and back ached from moving pots and crates, and had it really been only this morning that she had found the scorpion? Julia wanted nothing more than a warm bath and a good night's sleep.

She bid the others good night and started up the stairs, but a pounding on the front door stopped her.

"Gabrielle Martin, open this door at once."

Alice Laurent's voice was loud and sounded very angry. Julia came back down the stairs just as Gabi came into the entry hall, muttering about rude neighbors interrupting her game of piquet.

Luc was right behind her.

When Gabi opened the door, Alice pushed her way inside, forcing Gabi to take a step back. The neighbor's face was red, and her expression was furious. She looked at Luc and Julia but appeared too angry to even give a greeting. She glared at Gabi and took a step toward her. "This time you have gone too far, Gabrielle. How dare you do such a thing?"

Luc pushed his hands into his pockets and leaned a shoulder against the wall. He let out a breath, looking as if he'd like to escape, but he was trapped now that Alice had seen him.

"And what is it this time, eh? Has your hen laid in my garden again?" Gabi folded her arms and gave her neighbor a long-suffering sigh. "Really, how many eggs do the two of you eat?"

Julia rested one hand on the stair railing, wondering if a late-night argument was typical between the neighbors. Seeing how little the yelling affected Gabi and Luc, she figured it must be. She glanced up the stairs and wondered if she could make a discreet exit as she'd done earlier in the garden.

Alice pressed her fists against her eyes, then her mouth, looking as if she were too angry to even find words. "This . . . to do such a thing, it is despicable. I would never have thought you would stoop so low, Gabrielle."

Mathieu stepped in behind his wife, his face looking serious. His little dog came in as well and stood beside his master's feet. Mathieu nodded a greeting at the three of his neighbors and put a hand on his wife's shoulder. Whether to calm her or to support her, Julia could not be certain. But his presence seemed to make Gabi and Luc take Alice's diatribe more seriously.

Gabi's brows came together and her head tipped. She looked concerned.

Alice glanced at her husband. Her lip trembled.

Luc stood up straight. "What has happened?"

"You killed Fleur!" Alice pointed at Gabi with both hands. "She is so ill she can hardly walk. She will most likely not survive the night, and if she does, her milk will never be sweet again." She turned and fell, weeping, against her husband's shoulder.

Gabi and Julia gasped.

Mathieu dropped his cane, nearly hitting the dog. He held one hand against the doorframe for support and patted his wife's back with the other.

Gabi's expression was replaced by confusion. She glanced at Luc, who shrugged, confused as well. "What do you mean?" Her voice was concerned. "What happened to Fleur?"

"We found her tied to the sycamore by the south gate," Mathieu said, looking at them over his wife's scarf. His tone and expression were grave. "She'd been eating the—"

"Bracken fern," Gabi finished. She let out a heavy sigh and put a hand over her heart. "Oh, the poor thing."

Luc stepped closer, standing behind Gabi.

Julia's heart plummeted. Her head was light as the significance of what she was hearing became clear. She held tighter to the stair railing, feeling lightheaded. *No, it cannot be.*

"I know she eats your herbs." Alice turned away from her husband and back to glaring at Gabi, her face blotchy and wet. "She can't help it. It's in her nature. But to do such a thing to an innocent creature."

Gabi's face had gone pale. "I would never hurt an animal," she said.

"You want your chèvre to win at the fair," Alice said.

"No," Gabi said. "Not like this. I have no idea how Fleur came to be tied to the sycamore, but—"

"It was me," Julia said in a small voice, her heart beating so hard she could feel it in her limbs.

The four people and one dog turned to stare at her.

"You?" Mathieu asked.

Julia swallowed hard past the lump in her throat. "I found her in the garden and . . ." She looked down at her hands, finding it impossible to look at any of the faces staring at her, their expressions surely exhibiting the entire spectrum of anger, confusion, and—she was certain—disappointment. "I moved her away from the herbs but close to the gate so you would see her right away when you came looking. I tied the knot high in the tree so she wouldn't bite it." She glanced up. "I didn't know about the bracken fern."

"You." Alice pointed a shaky finger.

"I am so sorry, Madame Laurent." Julia's voice cracked. "I didn't realize the danger. I know nothing about caring for goats, and—"

"I should have known." Alice shook her head. "This is what happens when you let a stranger into your home, Gabrielle. You can't trust outsiders."

Alice turned fully toward Julia and leaned forward, glaring.

Julia cringed away. Her chest and ears burned.

"I imagine you thought it nothing at all to kill a simple goat." Alice's voice was pure vitriol. "You and your fancy city ways. What kind of person comes into a self-respecting town and murders an animal for fun? I'll tell you, an evil—"

"That's enough, Alice," Luc interrupted. He crossed the entryway and stood beside Julia. "Miss Weston made a mistake. It was a terrible accident, nothing more."

"An accident?" Alice pulled her lips together, and her body tightened, looking as if pressure were building and it was only a matter of time before she exploded.

Mathieu still had a hand on his wife's shoulder, but now he seemed to be restraining her rather than comforting her. "If mademoiselle says it was an accident . . . ," Mathieu said in a placating tone.

Luc leaned closer to Julia, and she wished for an irrational moment that he would put a hand on her shoulder, or that she could hold on to his arm—or hide behind him.

Gabi cleared her throat. "Come along to the kitchen. We will all feel better with some coffee and a nice piece of yogurt cake."

Alice was still staring at Julia. The anger in her eyes made Julia's breath come fast. "How will cake fix anything?" she spat. She pulled away from her husband's grasp with a jerk of her shoulder and folded her arms, frowning. She looked at Gabi. "You owe me a goat."

Gabi sucked in a breath.

"Coquette." Alice drew out the word, pronouncing each sound with emphasis.

Gabi pressed her fingers to her lips, and tears came into her eyes. She nodded.

"No," Julia said. She stepped around Luc. "Alice, I will buy you a goat. I have money."

Alice's brow raised as if the proposal interested her, but she still glared.

Julia pressed on. She would never allow Alice to take Gabi's beloved goat. "Luc will take me tomorrow to . . . wherever one goes to buy a goat." She looked up at Luc, pleading in her gaze. "Won't you?"

He rubbed his eyes. "It's not as easy as you think, Juliette. Purchasing livestock is more complicated than merely paying a visit to the local goat store."

Julia did not know how to answer. He was obviously being sarcastic, but she did not know how to find a new goat on her own. "Surely someone sells goats somewhere," she said.

Luc huffed through his nose. He shook his head. "Nowhere near here."

Julia's throat got even tighter. Buying a new goat was the only answer she could see to the problem she'd caused. "Please, Luc. I have to. This is my fault, and I can't let Gabi give up Coquette." She realized she'd taken hold of his hand with both of hers, but she did not let go, even though the action was extremely inappropriate for a young lady. "I can't do it without you. Please."

Luc looked at her for a moment, then looked toward the others in the entryway.

His aunt and neighbors stared back, waiting for his answer.

He glanced at her hands holding his, then lifted his gaze to Julia's. At last, Luc gave a long blink followed by a short nod.

Julia squeezed his hand. "Thank you." She released her grip and turned back to Alice. "I will fix this, Madame Laurent. And again, I am so very—"

"You choose the goat, Luc." Alice interrupted. "I trust you." She jerked her head toward Julia. "She'll not know the first thing about what to look for."

Luc nodded. "Oui."

"Taste the milk," Alice continued. "It must be sweet with no aftertaste."
He nodded again.

Alice gave a last glare to Julia. "I must go now and tend to my poor Fleur." She spun and stormed out the door.

Mathieu remained. "Gabrielle, I believe you mentioned yogurt cake . . ." He smiled.

"Oh yes. I will make a plate for you to take." She went into the kitchen.

Julia scratched the little dog's ears. She picked up Mathieu's cane and handed it to him. "Monsieur Laurent," she said in a timid voice. "I am truly sorry. I didn't mean—I would never hurt Fleur."

He took her hand. "Of course you wouldn't, ma chérie." He glanced back over his shoulder. "And Alice—she knows it too. She is just . . . upset."

He pressed a kiss to her hand and took the plate of cake Gabi brought. He leaned close to the cake and inhaled, closing his eyes. "Ah, my favorite. Merci, Gabrielle." Mathieu gave a pleased smile.

"I'll walk with you," Luc said. He took his coat from a peg by the door, sliding his hands into the sleeves. "See if there's anything I can do for the goat." He took the cake plate from Mathieu and held the door for the older man.

"Bonne nuit." Mathieu bowed to the ladies and turned carefully, leaning heavily on his cane as he walked. The little dog followed.

Luc started to follow but turned. "We will leave before dawn, Juliette. I'll knock on your door to wake you."

She nodded.

Once Gabi closed the door behind him, Julia sank down onto the bottom step of the staircase. "Oh, Gabi. What have I done?" She rested her elbows on her knees and sank her head onto her arms.

Fredric wound between her feet.

"It was an accident, Juliette. You must not feel responsible. You thought to help."

"But that poor animal." Julia spoke without lifting her head. "To think that she's suffering because of my ignorance." She turned her head to the side and glanced at Gabi. "The sycamore tree is right beside the gate. How is it that Fleur never ate the bracken fern before?"

"She would normally avoid any plant with shiny leaves. Animals—they can smell when something is harmful. But when she was tied right beside it and had no other choice—goats do not always make wise decisions." Gabi gave a partial smile.

Julia didn't feel any better. Her small action had such far-reaching consequences and affected both households. "And Luc—he cannot be pleased to spend another day away from his olives because of me, especially after the mess I made in the nursery, and then surprising him in his studio—"

"You saw his studio?" Gabi asked.

Julia straightened. She lifted the cat onto her lap, stroking his fur, and nodded, still feeling utterly miserable. "I took out one of the crates from the parlor, for storage."

Gabi's eyes had brightened considerably. "What did you think?"

"Luc's paintings are . . . they are completely splendid," Julia said. "More than splendid. It is—he is . . ." She paused trying to think of words to describe how very remarkable Luc's talent was. "My father—perhaps you know already—is the *Commissaire Expert des Beaux-Arts Anglais.* I know art. I've seen it, studied it my entire life, so I am not simply flattering." She turned her knees toward Gabi, setting a hand on the other woman's arm, wanting her to understand the significance of what she was saying. "Luc is more than simply a person with a talent for drawing and an eye for color. He possesses . . . the *je ne sais quoi* that separates the artist from the genius. It is not something a person can describe in words, but when one looks at Luc's paintings"—she glanced at the painting on the wall behind Gabi—"it is felt deep in one's soul."

"Oui," Gabi whispered, her eyes shining. "I know it."

"Luc's paintings should be on a museum wall," Julia said. "They should be appreciated, studied, experienced . . . not just set on the ground of his storage shed. They are exceptional."

Gabi nodded.

"He should be among the artists in the Grand Palais, representing France," Julia said. "But he keeps his work hidden away. Why?"

"You'll have to ask him," Gabi said.

"I do not think he will tell me." Julia gave a small shrug, feeling again the weight of the trouble she'd caused. "I imagine he regrets rescuing me from the Rivulet train station."

"I am certain that is not so," Gabi said. "Luc seems rather surly, but he has the most compassionate heart of anyone I know." One side of her mouth tugged up in a smile. "He just has trouble showing it. I suppose it's how he protects himself."

Julia thought of how he'd ridden all day to send a telegram for a person he'd just met, putting his new seedlings at risk. How he watched over his aunt even though she did not believe she needed it and had brought home a wet stranger who'd gotten onto the wrong train. The idea that his gruff demeanor was simply a mask made sense when compared to his actions. She smiled, turning back to rest her chin in her hands. "But my mistakes these past days would push even the most patient person to the edge of their tolerance."

Gabi chuckled and put an arm around Julia's shoulders. "You are too hard on yourself, ma chérie. You will see; it will all work out. Tomorrow, you and Luc will be back in Riv with the new goat, and Alice will be happy, which will make Mathieu happy." She gave an exaggerated sigh. "And I will have peace with my neighbor again."

"And you will keep Coquette," Julia said.

"Oui." Gabi rested her head on Julia's shoulder. "Merci, Juliette."

Julia tipped her head, leaning it on Gabi's. She felt warm at the woman's affection, and very loved, in spite of the trouble she'd caused. After today's disasters, Julia thought she was the last person anyone in Rivulet should be thanking. But Gabi's words gave her hope. Tomorrow would be better, and she promised herself she'd set everything right, and nobody would regret her visit to Provence.

The wiggly feeling came back into her stomach.

Especially not Luc.

CHAPTER TEN

THE EASTERN SKY HAD BARELY a tinge of purple when Julia followed Luc outside to the farm wagon. Gabi had provided a coat for Julia and packed a basket of food. Standing in the front hall in her nightclothes, she'd explained to Julia in a sleepy voice that there was a valley to the north with goat dairies, but to get there, they would need to go around the mountains. It would be close to noon by the time they arrived.

Julia climbed onto the wagon's bench with Luc's assistance. She secured her handbag on her arm, and as they rode, her eyes grew accustomed to the dim. Time passed, but Julia had no way of knowing how long they had been traveling, since it was still too dark to see either of her timepieces. But at least the road ahead was visible—for the most part. When she glanced to the side, she saw only Luc's silhouette in the darkness. His communication this morning had consisted of one-word answers and grunts, and she was not certain whether he was tired or annoyed at the inconvenience of another errand taking him away from his work.

Julia pulled the coat tighter around herself, shivering as a cool breeze hit and wishing she'd brought a blanket to put over her legs. She closed her eyes but did not fall asleep—the wagon's bench was too hard, the road too bumpy.

The silence was broken by the occasional noise from the horse and the crunch of the wheels on the gravel road. A few times, they passed a farmhouse in the brightening morning, but Julia still hadn't seen another person. The silence felt heavy and uncomfortable, and she finally could take it no longer.

"It's a lovely sunrise, don't you think?" She cringed at the inelegance of her statement.

Luc glanced at her and then toward the pink-and-purple sky. He made an affirmative-sounding grunt.

Julia wasn't about to let them lapse back into the awkward silence. "I think we are in for a nice day, don't you?"

He grunted again.

Apparently, Luc was not interested in early-morning conversation. Julia gave it one more attempt. "Do you travel to Greece often, Luc?"

"No."

She sighed, realizing she was destined to spend the entire day sitting beside a person who was determined to ignore her. She considered how she might make the time pass more quickly. Perhaps she could count the trees they passed or play a number game in her head.

"The trip last week was my first," Luc said after a long pause.

Julia started. His voice sounded loud after the quiet. "Oh," she said, not about to let the conversation dwindle. "And how did you find it?"

"Hot."

Julia could think of no response. The silence returned, and she shifted in her seat, thinking how nice it would feel to sit on a cushion. She watched the sky lighten until at last the sun appeared and the shadows receded as it rose higher. Farmland surrounded them, and it seemed everything in Provence was in bloom. Fields of lavender spread over hills like blankets set among the blossoming orchards and vineyards, the flowers filling the air with their fragrance. They were drawing closer to the rocky mountains. Atop one, Julia could see a city built of stone on the rounded peak.

Luc cleared his throat. He scratched the back of his neck and glanced at her. "I hear l'Exposition Universelle is very . . . ah . . . very impressive."

"Yes," Julia said, feeling a rush of excitement. Her father had prepared for years for the World's Fair, and his descriptions of its development over the past months had filled her with anticipation. "Did you know they have created an entire Egyptian village where one might ride a camel or take tea in a Bedouin tent?"

"I did not know that," Luc said.

"I hear even the shah of Persia is expected to attend."

Luc gave a nod but didn't seem particularly impressed by the rumor.

"And, of course, there is an Aztec Temple in the Mexican pavilion," Julia continued, not allowing his lack of enthusiasm to dampen her own. "Jules Massenet has composed a brand-new opera for the event. My father told me there are miles and miles of displays and exhibits and performers. Even sporting events and carnival rides, if one is interested in that sort of thing, and if one becomes tired from all the walking, an electric moving sidewalk will take you from place to place." She stopped when her voice ran out of breath, looking at her companion eagerly. Surely one could not help but be thrilled by the aspect of such a spectacle.

Luc nodded. "It sounds enjoyable."

He may have been speaking sarcastically, but if that was the case, she ignored it. She was far too excited. "And the art." Julia clasped her hands. This was the element of the exhibition for which her father had worked so tirelessly. "A gathering of the greatest works of the greatest artists in the world, all in one place—no museum can compete."

Luc seemed even quieter than before.

"My father said France has the most impressive presentation of all. Meissonier, Manet, Bouguereau . . ." She glanced at Luc, then took a breath. "You belong among them."

He scowled. He clicked his tongue at the horse, flicking the reins.

But he was trapped with her here, on this wagon seat, and she took advantage of his inability to walk away from something he found uncomfortable. "Luc, your art—"

"Non, Juliette." His voice was low, but Julia thought it sounded sad rather than angry.

"I know what I am saying. I've traveled with my father since I can remember. He's taught me to recognize the difference between good and remarkable art. Your paintings . . . Why do you keep such talent hidden away?"

"I have my reasons." Luc kept his gaze fixed on the horse.

"Do you worry that it is not good enough? That some might criticize? There are always those who will find fault." She turned toward him as much as she could on the wagon seat without losing her balance, wanting to give emphasis to her words. "Luc, you must believe me when I tell you this talent, *your* talent, is rare, and you should reveal it to the world."

"I will not." His words cracked in the air. This time, his voice was angry, leaving no room for argument.

Julia sighed, sitting back in the wagon seat. Luc didn't understand. Or he didn't trust her judgment. Frustration made her clench her teeth as she thought about how selfish he was being. Both he and Gabi would benefit from the profits if he sold his paintings. She had no doubt that once her father saw Luc's work, he would speak to his French counterpart and the paintings would receive a place of honor in the Grand Palais des Beaux-Arts. Julia imagined how proud Colonel Weston would be of her discovery. But as soon as she had the thought, a burning guilt stung her throat. She wasn't simply thinking of her father's approval but of Luc. The man's house was in shambles, he'd been forced to sell part of his family's farm, and the answer to all of his problems was sitting unappreciated in a storage building. She wanted people to know, but even more than that, she wanted Luc to realize that his work was special. The solution was so obviously simple.

"Shall we see what's in Gabi's basket?" Luc asked after a long silence.

Julia glanced at him. The glower was gone, and for that she was glad. She turned in the seat and reached back toward the basket, wishing there was something to hold on to as she did. Until two days ago, she had never ridden in a farm wagon, and she found the vehicle to be not only uncomfortable but unsafe as well. The seat sat high in the front, with no railing before it and only a low back behind. As she reached, the wagon went over a bump, causing her to lose balance. She grabbed on to Luc's arm to keep from falling into the wagon bed.

He pulled on the reins. "Perhaps a picnic is a safer proposition."

The pair climbed out of the wagon, and Julia was relieved for a chance to stretch out her legs and back. Her heart still beat rather fast from her near-fall. A glance at her two timepieces showed it was nine o'clock, long past the time for breakfast. She took off her coat, glad the morning had grown warm.

"Ground's rocky," Luc said after glancing around the area. "We can eat in the wagon." He stepped onto the running board and swung his leg over the side of the wagon. Then he reached down a hand to help Julia to do the same.

The step was high. She took his hand, held her skirts, and clumsily put her foot on the running board.

Luc pulled as she stepped up, placing his other hand on her waist to steady her when she almost fell against him, and hauled her over the side of the wagon.

Julia's face burned—both at Luc's closeness and the inelegance of it all. She kept her chin high, trying to look unaffected by his touch, and sat, knees to the side, arranging her skirts around her legs, as she imagined was the proper manner to sit for a picnic in a farm wagon. She pulled out the basket from the shady place beneath the wagon seat.

Luc sat across from her, resting his back against the side of the wagon, one leg bent, and the other stretched out next to her.

She took the cloth from the basket and, seeing the abundance of food within, grinned. "Gabi certainly will not allow us to go hungry." She laid out the cloth on the wagon bed and set out plates, cups, a knife, bread, cheese, a tin of sardines, a bowl of tapenade, a bottle of wine, and the remainder of the yogurt cake.

Luc's brow rose, and he shook his head. "She sends only a sandwich when I travel alone."

Julia cut a slice of bread and offered it to Luc, then cut one for herself and spread on some cheese. She leaned back against the wagon side and took a bite, the taste of the chèvre reminding her of the reason for the journey. A lump grew in her throat, and it became hard to swallow. "How did you find Fleur last night?" Shame made it difficult to even raise her eyes to Luc's gaze, but she darted a glance at him.

He brushed a crumb from the corner of his mouth. "She's ill. She'll probably not—"

"Oh." Julia covered her mouth, a fresh rush of emotion pushing on her eyes.

"Nobody blames—" Luc grimaced. "Nobody believes you intended deliberately to harm the animal," he corrected.

Julia nodded, not trusting herself to speak.

He bumped her knee with his leg, giving a smile. "It will be well. You'll see. You're making things right."

Julia nodded. The ache in her throat eased somewhat, but she still felt embarrassed for her dreadful mistake. And something about Luc's soft smile made the emotions feel even more muddled. She picked at her bread and looked around, hoping to change the subject. Beneath the wagon seat was an umbrella. Julia leaned to the side and lifted it. "I hope this wasn't here when we rode from the train station." She forced her voice to sound light.

Luc swallowed his bread and smirked. "Do you think I wouldn't have mentioned it when you were so wet?"

She shrugged. "I don't know if I'd put it past you."

"Gabi sent it today." He nodded toward the umbrella. "Said it will rain this afternoon."

Julia looked up at the clear sky. "Surely not."

"I'd never bet against Gabi when it comes to predicting the weather." Luc wrapped the bread and put it back into the basket.

Following suit, Julia helped him pack away the rest of the food. "But there's not one cloud in the entire sky."

"Gabi's knees ache when a storm's on the way," Luc said. He swung himself over the side of the wagon and landed on the ground.

Julia tucked the basket back beneath the seat with her coat. She stood, brushing crumbs from her skirt, and debated for a moment whether it would be easier to climb over the back of the wagon seat or to jump down to the ground and climb back up. Though both options seemed equally graceless, she chose the latter. She lifted one leg over the side of the wagon, turned around, and eased downward. The running board was lower than she'd estimated, and her other leg slipped as she tried to get her footing.

Luc caught her around the waist, holding her up as she swung over the other leg.

Her back brushed against his chest, and she felt his breath on her cheek as he set her down on the ground.

She turned, and her hands settled on his chest as she caught her balance. She looked up to thank him, but his eyes caught hers, and her words froze in her mouth.

Luc's hands stilled on her waist, and for an instant, she was enveloped in his arms. His eyes softened, and his gaze flicked to her lips.

Fluttering threatened to tear apart Julia's stomach, and at once, panic stole her thoughts. She pulled away, mumbling a thanks to Luc for his assistance, and climbed up into the seat at the front of the wagon with shaking hands. Her cheeks burned, but this time, the heat wasn't caused by embarrassment from her near-fall. She could feel exactly where Luc had touched her, even though it had been for merely an instant. Her breath was light and her pulse heavy as she settled into the seat. And when Luc climbed up, she was unusually aware of how close he sat beside her. The air between them felt tense and alive, as if it were somehow filled with Mr. Edison's electricity. Luc flicked the reins, and his arm came dangerously close to brushing hers. Her skin tingled with goose pimples at the thought.

She breathed steadily to calm herself. And as they continued on toward wherever one goes to purchase a goat, Julia was for once grateful for the quiet as her mind turned over both their accidental embrace and the intensity of her reaction to it.

CHAPTER ELEVEN

The remainder of the morning passed in a silence that was a different type of uncomfortable. Julia found herself acutely aware of every movement Luc made. Each time he cleared his throat, shifted, even breathed, she was conscious of it. And at times, she hoped his movements would result in a brush against her arm or that his knee might bump hers. The entire side of her body tingled with anticipation of an accidental touch, to the point that when the wagon finally drew to a stop, Julia ached from the longing.

"You can remain here if you'd like," Luc said. "I'll inquire at the farmhouse."

Julia's face flushed at the sound of his voice, and the embarrassment of her reaction made her flush even more. She nodded.

Luc climbed down and knocked on the door.

A cloud moved in front of the sun, casting a shadow. A cool breeze blew, and Julia looked up, surprised to see clouds and grateful for a distraction. She needed to pull herself together and stop with these silly thoughts. How had her mind become so addled?

She closed her eyes and leaned back, letting the cool breeze wash over her. The air smelled fresh, even with the scent of animals.

A raindrop hit her cheek. Then another.

Julia turned around on the seat. She leaned precariously over the back of the bench and pulled out the umbrella from beneath. And her coat.

By the time Luc returned a moment later, the rain was falling steadily.

"No goats for sale," he said, climbing up to the bench. "But madame told me where we might find some."

Julia moved the umbrella so it covered Luc as well. She held it between them, angling her shoulder so she wasn't leaning against him, although the small diameter of the umbrella made it nearly impossible for the two not to squeeze together. She had a fleeting thought that this was perhaps Gabi's intention but pushed it away. Surely not.

The dairy the woman from the farmhouse directed them to was nearly an hour farther along the road, and when the pair climbed out of the wagon and walked to the farmhouse door, they had to dodge muddy puddles the entire way.

Luc knocked, and a moment later, a round man with a red nose opened the door. He squinted, making the pronounced wrinkles around his eyes even more pronounced, and eyed them suspiciously. "*Bonser?*"

Julia wondered if the elderly man had a speech impediment. She adjusted the handbag on her arm, not wanting to stare and appear rude.

"*Cossí va?*" Luc said.

"*Ben.*"

Luc spoke for a long moment, and the man answered. Julia realized they must be speaking a regional Provençal dialect. She listened carefully, picking out a few words, but could not follow the conversation.

The old man visibly relaxed as they spoke. He glanced at Julia and asked Luc a question Julia didn't understand.

Luc's answer made the man smirk.

They spoke for a moment longer, until finally the old man nodded. "*Monsen, madòna.*" He pointed with his hand, palm up, and jerked his head to the side, indicating for the pair to follow him.

Luc took the umbrella and offered Julia his arm.

She put her hand into the bend of his elbow, feeling a tingle move through her fingers, and they started down the muddy path after the dairy owner.

For an elderly man, he walked surprisingly fast.

"What did he say?" Julia asked Luc in a low voice.

Luc's lips twitched. "He said it's early in the season to buy a goat."

Julia suspected he wasn't telling her the entire truth. "And . . . what else?" She was getting winded from walking so fast.

"I told him you were determined to have a goat today, and—" He smirked again.

"Yes?" Julia tugged on his arm.

"He said he understands how it is. When his wife sets her mind to something, he knows he'll have no peace until she gets it."

Julia huffed. "And naturally, you explained that I don't simply want a goat on a whim. We need one." She glanced up and saw that his smirk remained. "And you did tell him I'm not actually your wife."

Luc didn't answer.

"Luc . . ."

"I figured I'd let him think what he likes. If it helps us get a goat, then so be it."

A tingling spread up the back of Julia's neck and across her face. "But . . ."

"He offered his congratulations," Luc said.

Julia stopped and folded her arms, but her defiant gesture was short-lived when Luc and the umbrella moved on without her and the rain showered over her scarf and dress. She hurried to catch back up with Luc, grabbing on to his arm. "I don't think it is the right thing to do, misleading this man like that."

He adjusted the umbrella to cover her. "Rural people are . . . traditional," he said. "Old-fashioned." His smile remained, but he was no longer teasing. "He may have a different reaction to the pair of us traveling together unchaperoned if he knew the truth."

"Oh," Julia said, the blush she'd fought against all day returning with a vengeance. She hadn't even considered the impropriety of their journey.

"So come along, *mon plus cher amour*." The tease was back in his voice, but it was gentle, as if asking her to laugh along with him. "Shall we choose a goat?"

Though it was spoken in jest, the endearment caught her off guard, and she could think of no reply. She kept her eyes on the ground as they walked down the rocky path.

They reached a paddock filled with goats and joined the farmer beneath the overhanging roof of a small barn. Little goat kids ran about, kicking and jumping between the larger animals. They called out with bleats.

Julia clapped her hands and laughed at their antics. She couldn't help it. The baby goats were utterly delightful.

The farmer spoke to Luc, pointing among the animals, and Julia didn't even try to understand what they were saying. She was much too captivated by the little goats.

They kicked hooves that appeared too large for their bodies into the air, sometimes falling over from the sheer effort as they bounded throughout the paddock. One little goat jumped onto the back of another, balancing on what appeared to be the tips of his toes before he was bucked off. He bounded away through the mud, and two others followed.

The farmer entered the paddock and brought a few of the older goats over to Luc. He tied them to the fence, pointing out various features, then left the paddock to go into the barn for a tin cup. When he returned, he crouched down and reached through the slats of the fence to fill the cup with a bit of milk from one of the goats.

Luc took a sip and offered the cup to Julia.

She looked at it, wondering when it had last, if ever, been washed. But she remembered Alice and fought against the urge to wipe off the rim. She took a sip of the warm milk, and they repeated the process with the other goats' milk.

"What do you think?" she asked Luc after the fourth sample. She could honestly not tell a difference in the flavor.

He pointed to a light-brown goat with white spots on her back. "That one has the sweetest milk."

Julia nodded and looked closer at the animal. "Is she to be Alice's goat, then?"

"The decision is yours," Luc said.

She smiled and took the umbrella from Luc, walking to the fence for a closer look at the animal. Julia had no idea what made a good nanny goat, but she wanted to make a responsible decision and look over the animal for any obvious defects. The goat's hooves and legs were muddy, and she produced a pungent smell that was only strengthened by the rain. The nanny gave a bleat, and her long tongue hung from the side of her mouth. As goats went, she was perfect.

"We will take her," Julia said.

The men talked again, presumably discussing the price, and Julia returned to stand beneath the barn's overhang.

The farmer went back into the paddock and untied the goat, bringing her to the gate. Two of the little kids followed with their delightful little bounces, their back legs moving in different directions than their front.

The farmer led the goat through the gate, but the animal drew back, fighting against him and bleating loudly. He gave a mighty pull, holding his leg out to stop the little ones from following. When he closed the gate, their bleats sounded like babies' cries.

"Wait." Julia tugged on Luc's arm as she realized what was happening. "Are they her babies?"

"Looks like it," he said.

"I didn't realize she is a mother. And they are so small. We can't separate them."

The farmer called out a question.

Luc stepped out into the rain to explain.

Julia went to the gate and crouched down, holding the umbrella overhead and patting the crying goats. She wished she could comfort them. "Don't worry, little ones. I won't take away your mother." She joined Luc and the farmer. "We will have to find another goat. One without babies."

Luc folded his arms and sighed. "Juliette, if a goat is producing milk, it means she's given birth."

The farmer's smirk returned as he looked between the two. "Don't worry, *madòna*," he said, speaking in a thick accent. "I take good care of the kids."

The mother goat bleated and strained to get to the gate.

The baby goats cried out for her.

Julia's heart ached at the sight. There was only one thing to do. "We will take all of them." She gave a nod, satisfied that she'd come up with the best solution.

The farmer looked as if he were holding back a laugh. He looked at Luc as if waiting for him to explain to his confused wife how goat husbandry worked.

Luc rubbed his forehead. "Juliette, the kids will be cared for. It is usual for her to leave them."

"There is nothing usual about growing up without a mother," Julia said. She'd not meant for her voice to crack. She swallowed. "I can't do it to them. I won't." She crouched back down and patted the wet baby goats.

Luc was silent, and when Julia glanced up, she saw that he was watching her.

He rubbed the back of his neck again, and after a long moment, he spoke again to the farmer.

The elderly man listened, then let out a hearty laugh. He clasped Luc's shoulder, shaking his head as if in sympathy for the poor newlywed's plight.

Julia didn't imagine she would have been pleased to understand his words.

Half an hour later, the rain still poured down as they started back along the muddy road toward Rivulet. Julia held the umbrella over herself and Luc, and three goats slid around in the bed of the wagon.

With every bump or bleat, Julia twisted around on the bench, worried a goat had fallen or gotten free from the ropes and jumped over the side.

"They'll settle down in a bit, won't they?" she asked.

Luc shrugged. "I've never driven an entire goat family through the rain before."

"Well, I'm glad we brought them all. Look how happy they are to be together." She watched over Luc's shoulder as the babies tried to move around the crowded space, their hooves slipping on the boards. "I do wish they'd just sit down though."

She turned back around, settling against the back of the seat. "I didn't realize both Fleur and Coquette were mothers. What happened to their babies?"

"Mathieu's brother, Benoit, is a breeder. Every winter, he brings his billy goat to town. Sometimes he buys, sometimes he sells. Mathieu used to keep a large herd, but now, just Fleur for milk and a few others to manage the weeds."

"Why did we not go to Benoit for a goat today?"

"His farm is too far away. Near Pertuis."

Julia nodded, and the conversation died away. She wished the rain would stop. Luc had to maneuver the horse around deep mud puddles, and the ride seemed to go much slower. Her arm was getting tired, so she held the umbrella in the other hand for a time.

The patter of rain on the canvas overhead had a lulling effect, and Julia's eyes drifted closed. She jerked them open when the umbrella dropped and rain hit her face. She looked at both time pieces and saw they had been traveling only for two hours. Even with her coat and the umbrella, she was wet and cold. It seemed they were in for an uncomfortable afternoon.

Hearing a rustling sound, she turned and saw one of the little goats had gotten free. He was probing his nose into their lunch basket.

"No, that is not for you." Julia turned around again, knelt on the bench, and leaned over the seat back, trying to push the goat away from the food. "Go back—"

The wagon went over a bump, and Julia bounced, lost her grip, dropped the umbrella, and plunged forward.

Luc caught her, saving her from crashing down into the wagon bed, but doing so meant he had to let go of the reins. He pulled her up onto the seat, made certain she was seated properly, and reached down for the reins.

Before he could grab them, the horse veered on its own to avoid a mud puddle. The wagon followed suit, but the turn was too sharp. The wheels got too close to the side and slipped off the road. Luc pulled the horse back to the center of the track, but the damage had been done. The rear wheel slipped farther down into a muddy ditch, and the wagon jerked to a stop, pulling the horse backward and sending the goats sliding forward.

Luc gritted his teeth. He flicked the reins, and the horse strained but could not pull the wagon back onto the road. The wheel slid down farther, making the entire vehicle—and all its inhabitants—lean back and to the side.

Luc jumped down to the road, his boots crunching on the gravel, and walked around the back of the wagon.

Julia climbed down to join him, holding her hands over her head in a useless attempt to keep the rain off her face. The three goats watched over the side of the wagon bed. "Perhaps we should push," she suggested.

Luc glanced at her. He stepped into the mud, frowning when he sank down. He braced his shoulder against the back of the wagon. "When I yell, pull on the horse's harness. Make sure she walks straight forward, keeping the wheels in line."

Julia nodded and tried not to allow her worry to show. She didn't know the first thing about leading a horse, but she figured it must be very similar to leading a goat. She climbed up out of the ditch and stood in front of the horse, finding it to be larger than she'd remembered now that the two were facing one another and standing so close. Water dripped from the animal's mane and caught in droplets on her eyelashes. Julia took hold of the harness on either side of the horse's neck. The leather smelled wet and slipped a bit in her fingers.

"*Allez*," Luc called.

"*Allez, cheval*," Julia said to the horse. She stepped back, pulling with all her strength.

The horse lowered his head, pushing back on his hooves as he strained. The cart groaned and budged the slightest bit, but it didn't roll forward.

A splat sounded, and Luc cursed.

Julia let go of the harness. She rushed back to the rear of the wagon, stepping gingerly along the edge of the ditch. Luc had slipped and was on his hands and knees in the mud.

She bent to help him, but he jerked his arm away.

He pushed himself up to kneel and wiped his dirty hands on his trousers. His face was red, and he looked furious.

At that moment, the little goat that had gotten loose and invaded the picnic basket jumped down from the wagon and landed on Luc's shoulder. It balanced for a moment, then bounced away.

Luc lunged for the goat but missed, and his hands splashed back into the mud. He got to his feet, tearing his boots free and stomping out of the ditch. "Juliette, you have brought nothing but bad luck!" He sputtered the words, rainwater splashing off his hat.

Julia drew back, feeling as if she'd been struck. A rock clogged her throat, and her eyes stung. She slapped her hand over her mouth as a sob pushed its way through. The truth of his statement washed over her, and she rushed away before Luc could see the effect it had.

She sank down onto a wet rock and buried her face in her arms, sobs fighting free in spite of her efforts to hold them back. Luc was right. She had brought nothing but bad luck since she'd stepped off the train in Igney-Avricourt. She'd avoided the facts, blaming Nicholas or the absent Rivulet stationmaster or even Fleur, but the truth was good intentions were not enough. Her judgment wasn't to be trusted. She was everything she tried so hard to convince her father that she wasn't.

She heard Luc come to stand before her but didn't lift her head. She wished she could sink through the ground. She was done making excuses. Done thinking she knew what was best for everyone else. Luc didn't deserve the trouble she'd caused. Nobody did.

His boots creaked as he squatted down in front of her. "*Pardonnez-moi*, Juliette. I was frustrated. I shouldn't have said such a thing." His voice was low and gentle. "Please forgive me."

"But you are right," she said, her voice coming in gasps. "I've made a mess of everything." She heard a bleat and looked up.

Luc held the baby goat. He set the animal down, holding on to its rope so it didn't run away again.

She tried to smile, but her lip quivered. She shook her head. "You're right. And my father is right. I always think I know what's best. I think I can do things myself, but I can't. That is why he insisted on a chaperone."

Luc turned around to sit on the rock beside her. He tugged the goat along with him. "The poor Frau Maven you left asleep on the Orient Express while you got on the wrong train?" He bumped her arm softly with his as if sharing a joke and hoping she'd laugh.

"That is precisely why I needed a chaperone in the first place." She wiped her wet cheeks with her fingers. "I took the wrong train, got off at the wrong station, disarranged the nursery, killed Fleur, and now here we are, in the rain with the wagon stuck in the mud, and three goats." She waved a hand toward the wagon, where the mother goat and the other baby chewed on the umbrella. "*Je suis incompétent*," she said. Frustration made her words come out as a whine. "I try to do things right, to help and make things better, but I just make it all worse. I ruin everything."

"Not everything." Luc offered his handkerchief.

It was wet, and between the rain and her tears, Julia didn't think it would make much of a difference. But she took it, appreciating the thought anyway.

"You don't ruin everything," Luc continued. "I haven't seen Gabi so happy for a long time."

"I only straightened her kitchen," Julia said.

"And it made all the difference." The goat was pulling on the rope. Luc gave it a tug to bring the animal close. "You saved a goat family from separation," he continued. "And planted the olive seedlings for me."

"But—" Julia began to protest but stopped when Luc held up a hand.

"Not to mention, I quite enjoyed your train-station cake."

She gave a small laugh, appreciating that he was attempting to make her feel better. "I need to remember that I don't always know what's best for everyone," she said, turning around the folded handkerchief in her hands. "I just want so badly to help, but—"

"That is something you must never apologize for," Luc said. He stretched his legs out in front of him and sat quietly, giving her time to compose herself.

Julia considered what he said. The words were simple, and perhaps the warmth in her chest had more to do with the man who said them. She sighed, resting her cheek on her hand. It had been years since she'd cried so hard, and it had made her tired. "What do we do now?" she asked. The problem had not gone away. They were both soaking wet, Luc was covered in mud, and the wagon was still stuck.

He blew out a breath and looked back along the road. "We passed a farmhouse about a mile ago. Hopefully, someone there can help."

The idea of walking so far was discouraging, but to get out of the rain, Julia thought she'd do just about anything. She looked toward the wagon. "What about . . . ?"

"I'll bring the horse," he said. He put the rope in her hand. "You're bringing the goats."

CHAPTER TWELVE

THE TWO HUMANS, ONE HORSE, and three goats trekked down the muddy road. The sounds of crunching footsteps on the wet gravel and the pattering of rain were accompanied by the occasional bleat.

Julia had found it difficult to manage all three goats at once and had finally tied the kids' ropes to their mother's. They seemed content to follow along if she could keep the mother moving. But the goat apparently had other plans, tugging the rope toward every patch of shrubs they passed. And when she did, she pulled her two babies and Julia along with her.

"Come along, Honey. No stopping," Julia said. She dug her heels in and held the lead firmly. The rope was slippery, and one of the baby goats stumbled as it splashed through a muddy puddle. All of this would be much easier if it were not raining.

"Honey?" Luc asked.

"Oui. It is the English word for *le miel*. I thought she was rather honey-colored," Julia said. "At least, most of her." She used both hands to pull the goats. "And in English, it is also a term of endearment."

Luc grunted. He walked steadily with the horse, rain dripping from his hat rim.

"Do you think Alice will like the name?" Julia asked. The goat stopped again, pulling Julia's arm backward.

"Watching you lead those animals, I'm surprised you're considering any kind of endearment."

"It's not their fault it's raining," she said, pulling the rope over her shoulder and holding on to it with both hands. She leaned forward as she walked, using her leg strength to keep the animals moving.

When she glanced at Luc again, she thought his lips twitched. No doubt he wanted her to ask for help, but she would not. The goats were her responsibility. And she could be just as stubborn as Honey.

They reached the farmhouse at last, stopping at a break in the low wall that led into a well-tended garden. Julia made certain to keep the goats back, near the road, away from the herbs and flowers. Asking someone for assistance while one's animals destroyed their yard seemed a poor idea.

The mother goat found a patch of grass beside the wall to munch on.

The baby goats found their mother.

Luc squinted, looking at the house and the vineyard beyond. A stone building with a wide door that appeared to be a barn stood on one side of the garden.

She glanced at him, wondering what he was looking at. "What is it?"

"Young vines," he said.

"They do look small."

Luc nodded. "In the spring, they are cut back to the main stem before the sap starts to rise. That is why they look small. But the stems, they are slender. From America, I imagine." He tied the horse's lead to a metal ring in the wall.

"Why would the vines be American?" Julia asked. She leaned back against the stone wall, letting the rope slacken as the goats ate. Her arms ached from pulling them. The rain continued steadily, but it had lightened to a drizzle.

"American vines are resistant to the phylloxera aphid," Luc said. He pulled the knot tight and patted the horse. "Though it's still unproven, it's thought American vines caused the blight in the first place. Wine growers brought the vines from California for grafting, and they were immune to the pests that killed the European vines."

"It must have been terrible," Julia said. From what she'd heard of the blight, it had plagued the vineyards since before she was born, ruining many who had been in the wine business for generations.

"It was," Luc said. "A vine in the middle of a healthy vineyard would yellow and die without warning. Then the others around it would do the same. It spread fast, and nothing could stop it." He took Honey's lead rope from Julia and tied it to a ring on the other side of the wall's opening.

"You remember it?"

"The most devastating years were in my father's and grandfather's time. But the effects are still felt in Provence." He offered Julia his elbow.

"Are we pretending to be married again?" she asked.

"If you're amenable to it. I don't know these people."

"Very well." She took his arm, her heartbeat speeding up. She enjoyed the charade quite a lot but did not dare to say it.

"*Viens alors.*" Luc glanced at her, his lips pulling into a smirk. "Honey."

Julia's blush burned up her neck and over her cheeks.

When Luc knocked, the farmhouse door was opened by a young woman Julia estimated to be close to five years her senior. She held a baby on her hip and studied them with a cautious gaze. A small girl with dark curls peeked around the woman's skirts.

Luc explained their trouble, and the woman's face softened. She opened the door wider. "Madame, please come inside, out of the rain. Monsieur, my husband tends the vines. Go to him. He will be happy to help." She glanced toward the road. "You may put your animals in the pen, behind the house."

Luc thanked her. He glanced at Julia as if to make certain she was agreeable to being left with a stranger.

His concern gave her a thrill, and she looked away, embarrassed that yet another blush heated her face. She nodded. "I will be all right."

"Not to worry, monsieur. I will take good care of your wife." The woman smiled. She opened the door wider, and Julia stepped over the threshold into a main room that served as a kitchen, eating area, and parlor. The furnishings were simple and worn, but everything was clean.

Julia's skirts dripped, making a puddle on the stone floor.

The woman instructed her to leave her muddy boots beside the door. "I am Sylvie Deschamps."

"Julia W—" She stopped, her cheeks growing warm again. "Julia Paquet."

"*Bienvenue*, Madame Paquet." Sylvie stepped to the side, urging the small girl forward. "This is Élise."

"Bonjour, Élise."

"Bonjour," the girl said in a shy voice. She stepped back behind her mother.

"And here is little Adrien." Sylvie bounced the baby on her hip.

Adrien sucked on his fist, and Julia smiled.

She untied the wet knots in the laces of her boots, and by the time she stepped out of the boots and set them by the door, Sylvie had returned and handed her a towel. "I put dry clothes in the washroom." She motioned toward a door that led from the main room. "I think we are close to the same size. We can dry your dress by the fire."

"Merci," Julia said. In the washroom, she found clothes in a style very similar to those she'd borrowed from Gabi. Sylvie was a bit taller, and the skirts brushed the floor. Julia made certain she still had her wristwatch and hung the other timepiece around her neck. She wrung out her wet clothing and brought it back out to the hearth.

Sylvie had set up a wooden drying frame, and she laid Julia's clothes over it.

"Thank you again," Julia said.

"So much rain!" Sylvie tsked and shook her head. "But the grapes will be all the plumper for it."

"Your house is lovely," Julia said.

"Merci." Sylvie put a log into the fire.

Julia looked around with interest as she dried her hair with the towel. Much of the farmhouse's style reminded her of Gabi's. But there were distinct differences as well. Instead of cupboards and shelves overflowing with dishes and knickknacks, Sylvie had very few items for display. The things she did own appeared functional and meticulously taken care of, even if they were well used. Her home was simple, but Julia could see the woman took pride in it.

"You must be chilled," Sylvie said, motioning toward the kitchen table. "Come, sit. I will make *vin chaud*."

"Let me help you," Julia said, feeling uncomfortable with the prospect of being waited on, especially since she was the one imposing.

Sylvie considered for a moment, then handed Adrien to her. "Do you mind?" She shook out her arm and rubbed her back. "That one, he is becoming too heavy to carry all day." She leaned close to the baby and waggled a finger in pretend chastisement. "Your *maman's* arm is tired, mon cher."

Julia held the baby on her own hip, the same way she'd seen Sylvie do, wrapping an arm around him to keep him from falling. The baby was heavy, and after a few moments, she shifted him to her other hip, trying to imagine how difficult it must be to hold him as well as tend to the household chores.

"How old is he?" Julia asked.

"Nine months." Sylvie poured wine into a saucepan and lit the stove beneath it. She looked at the baby with fondness, then down at the little girl. "And Élise, tell Madame Paquet how old you are."

"Julia, please," Julia said. She directed her words to Élise and her mother, hoping to set the little girl at ease.

"And call me Sylvie," the woman said. She patted her daughter on the head. "Élise? Come, mon amour, don't be shy."

Élise poked out from behind her mother's skirts. "*Cinq*." She held up five chubby fingers.

"Quite a young lady," Julia said. Adrien squirmed, and she bounced him on her hip. "And this baby here." Julia pointed to a doll in a tiny cradle by the sofa. "Is she yours?"

"Oui." Élise took a few hesitant steps closer. "*Elle s'appelle Belle.*"

Julia squatted down to Élise's height, and then, feeling as if the baby's weight might cause her to lose her balance, she knelt and held Adrien in her lap.

Élise knelt beside her, holding Belle. She rocked the doll carefully and smoothed out its dress, then straightened the doll's pillow in the cradle.

Julia could see right away that she was a deliberate little girl with a serious mind. She smiled, recognizing aspects of herself in Élise's personality.

The smell of oranges and spices mixed with the hot wine filled the farmhouse, and a moment later, Sylvie brought her a mug. "This should warm you." She lifted the baby, kissing his cheeks. "Come along, little one. Time to sleep."

Julia stood, brushing off her skirts, and sat in a chair. It seemed as if the young mother was always moving from one task to the next. Julia wondered if she ever got the chance to sit in the middle of the afternoon and enjoy a mug of vin chaud. Probably not.

Sylvie took the baby into a bedroom, and while she was gone, Julia sipped the hot drink and watched Élise.

The young girl pretended to feed her doll from a toy bottle. She rocked Belle, humming quietly, and then set her in the little cradle, laying a blanket carefully over the stuffed body.

Julia smiled, feeling extremely content watching the girl. The home was tidy and pleasant. Her insides warmed with the hot drink. She only ever had vin chaud at Christmastime, and it was a delightful treat. She felt sleepy.

Sylvie came from the bedroom, closing the door quietly behind her. "At last." She gave an exaggerated sigh and smiled. "Now, a moment for maman." She poured herself a mug of the warm drink and joined Julia, resting back into the sofa.

Élise climbed up beside her, laying her head down on her mother's lap.

Sylvie ran her fingers over the little girl's hair. "Such blessings, these little ones. But they do leave a mother tired some days." She took a sip and looked at Julia over the rim of her mug. "You and your husband hope to have children soon?"

"Oh." Julia blinked, sitting straighter and clearing her throat. The question was so unexpected, and she had no idea how to answer.

Sylvie laughed. "By your blush, I can see you are still newly wed, non? I should have known based on the way monsieur looked at you."

"How he looked at me?" Julia asked, her voice sounding creaky. She could tell the blush wasn't going away anytime soon.

"Eh, oui." Sylvie winked. "Gentle eyes, adoring glances, the close way he watched you. He was so worried to leave you behind." She sighed and laughed again. "The look of a man newly in love."

Julia thought perhaps the woman had drunk too much wine. She tried to calm the shaking Sylvie's words caused and, in the end, leaned forward to set down her mug, lest she spill. "And your husband does not . . . ?" She figured if Sylvie could make so personal an inquiry to someone she'd just met, Julia would do the same. Besides, a part of her really wished to hear more about how Luc had looked at her.

"Oh, of course. Pierre and I, we love one another very much. But in the beginning, it is different. So much desire, the longing. You do not want to leave one another's sight. And when you are apart, you ache for each other." She put a hand on her heart. "*Très romantique.*"

"Oh my." Julia put a hand to her cheek. She didn't think it was possible to blush any deeper, but she was entirely wrong.

Élise raised her head and looked between the women with her nose wrinkled as if disgusted by the entire conversation.

Sylvie laughed, kissing her daughter's nose. "You will see one day, ma chérie, when you fall in love yourself."

Élise's lip curled, and she looked as if that was the last thing she intended to do.

Julia's hands had stopped shaking, but her insides had not. Sylvie of course had a misconception about the relationship between herself and Luc. But still, could what she said be true? Could Luc Paquet love her? The thought set off a reaction inside her that was both confusing and terrifying. And, if she were honest, hopeful.

But of course Luc didn't love her. He didn't even like her. She had been nothing but trouble to him from the moment she arrived in Rivulet. He'd told her only a few hours earlier that she'd brought him nothing but bad luck. And . . .

But what if it were true?

Her heart felt as if it melted, and she smiled, looking toward the window.

"Ah, you see?" Sylvie said. She rose and took Julia's mug with her own to the kitchen. "You miss him. But do not worry. Pierre will return him soon." She set the mugs in the washbasin. "Well, it's back to work, eh?"

"How can I help?" Julia asked, glad for a change of subject. Her thoughts were fanciful, and she was being silly to even entertain them. She looked around the snug little cottage but couldn't immediately see anything needing attention. "Do you need assistance preparing dinner?"

"Not for a little while yet." Sylvie pursed her lips and glanced toward a basket by the hearth. "I do have nuts to shell . . . but I'll not ask you to do that. Would you play with Élise instead? Between the baby and the housework, she gets less attention than she used to, and I know she would love to show you her drawings."

"Oh, are you an artist, Élise?" Julia asked.

The little girl studied Julia for a moment, then seemed to make up her mind. She went into a bedroom and brought out a large notebook and a wooden box.

She sat at the kitchen table, and Julia joined her.

Sylvie sat next to the fire and set to work cracking the shells off almonds with practiced movements and dropping the nuts into a bowl.

"May I?" Julia asked. Seeing Élise's nod, she opened the notebook and carefully turned the pages, commenting on the drawings the young girl had made.

The wooden box contained coloring pencils, and Julia could see that the child took good care of them. They were arranged in color order with a sharpener and a rubber eraser.

Élise had spent an exceptional amount of time on her pictures. Julia thought she would love to get such dedication from the young ladies at Frau Pichler's finishing school. Most of them rushed through a drawing assignment, just wanting to be finished. But not this girl.

Julia turned another page, recognizing a rendition of Élise's house. It was, of course, drawn in the simplistic manner of a child's skill. But she recognized an attempt at shading on one side of the chimney. The vineyard and the mountains beyond were colored in progressively lighter tones, showing a basic attempt to portray depth. Advanced for a child of her age.

Another page contained a portrait Julia guessed to be Sylvie. The proportions and spacing of the features were advanced as well.

Julia pointed out some of the places where she could see Élise had made an extra effort. "These are very good, Élise. My father works with famous artists all over the world. I have learned to recognize talent, and I can see you work extremely hard on your drawings. If you continue to do so, you will make a very fine artist."

Élise nodded thoughtfully. "And maybe *votre père* will work with me."

Julia smiled. "I hope that happens." It was a pity she and Luc wouldn't remain long enough for him to draw with Élise.

The young girl flipped to a page farther back in the notebook. "This is Adeline's cat." She turned the book toward Julia, showing a partially completed drawing. "Adeline is my cousin. But we have not been to her house for a long time. So I cannot finish the picture."

Julia nodded. "I see." She glanced toward the window and saw the rain had at last stopped completely. "Perhaps you might like to draw a baby goat."

Élise's face lit up. "I would like that very much!"

Once they obtained Sylvie's permission—with a promise to avoid mud puddles—Julia took the girl's hand, and the pair walked out to the animal pen, drawing supplies in tow.

Élise laughed when she saw the little goats. She stood beside the pen with her drawing pad and pencil box while Julia dragged over two wrought-iron chairs from an outdoor café set.

The chairs were damp, so Julia hurried back inside for a towel, and a few moments later, Élise sat with her pad on her lap, and Julia sat beside her, holding the pencils. "The mother is Honey," she said. "But the little ones don't have names yet."

"You might call the one with the black forehead and white face Guignol," Élise said.

"Like the puppet?"

"Oui." Élise spoke slowly, concentrating on her drawing. "I saw a Guignol show in Cavaillon. With Adeline." She looked up at the goats for a moment, then back at her paper. "The other one could be Spot. Because she has spots."

"Guignol and Spot." Julia thought the logic was sound.

"I am drawing Guignol," Élise said. "Because the black pencil is longer."

Julia watched the goats and the girl. She inhaled the smell of fresh rain and grape vines and flowers and imagined what it must be like to be Sylvie Deschamps. There were no houses closeby that Julia could see. Sylvie probably did not often have visitors. Was she lonely? Or did she find joy in caring for her home and family? Julia knew financial matters were always a concern for farmers. The blight had ruined thousands of vineyards, sending their owners to the cities for work. Did those who remained worry that such a disaster could happen again?

She looked beyond the pen, beyond the garden, to the vineyard, planted with young vines. Provence did not seem barren and desolate, as she'd thought when she'd ridden from the Rivulet train station. The people were happy. And in the air was a feeling of . . . hope. That's what made a man plant new vines from America or an old lady make the sweetest cheese or a girl draw pictures of a cat. Hope for the good things that life would bring if they poured their heart into the things they loved.

She considered Luc and the paintings hidden away in the storage building. Julia's heart grew heavy. She believed Luc cared about the orchard. But art was his passion. She'd seen it in his paintings. And Luc lacked that hope. If only she could find a way to give it to him.

CHAPTER THIRTEEN

THE SOUND OF HORSES' HOOVES and wagon wheels on the gravely road meant the return of the men. Julia resisted the impulse to jump up from her chair and run toward the road when she saw Luc. She waved instead.

Luc lifted a hand in return.

The man sitting beside him must be Monsieur Pierre Deschamps. Another horse followed the wagon, led with a rope. Julia assumed the men had used both animals to extricate the wagon.

"That is my papá," Élise said as the men climbed down from the wagon and led the horses toward the barn. Julia wasn't certain why Luc didn't leave his own horse hitched to the wagon, but perhaps he thought it needed a rest and maybe something to eat before they undertook the remainder of the journey.

"Your papá was very nice to help unstick the wagon," she said.

Élise nodded. "Papá helps me too."

Julia smiled at the girl. "That's what papás do, isn't it?" She stood. "Shall we return to the house? I think I will be leaving soon."

Élise's brow furrowed as she looked at her notebook. She sighed. "I didn't finish drawing Guignol." She handed the pencil to Julia to return to the box.

Julia carried the chairs back to their place in the garden and took the girl's hand to walk back to the house. They met the men coming from the barn, and Luc introduced her to Pierre Deschamps.

The man was shorter and wider than Luc, with a boyish face. He gave Julia a bright smile. "Ah, madame. So nice to meet you at last. Luc has told me such complimentary things about you."

Julia blushed. She glanced at Luc, then looked away quickly, feeling silly for the giddy reaction to Pierre's words. Naturally, Luc had attempted to maintain the charade of their marriage. And if Pierre was anything like his wife, he'd asked questions that had required personal answers, which Luc would have fabricated, of course.

Élise released Julia's hand and took her papá's. "I've been drawing goats with Julia," she said.

"C'est merveilleux, chérie!" Pierre said. "More of your beautiful pictures to admire. Come, you must show me."

Luc's clothing was covered in mud, and splatters were on his face and hat. He looked weary. "Oh dear," Julia said, grimacing as she looked him over.

"Eh, oui," Pierre said. "Extracting the wagon was no easy feat. But do not worry, madame. Sylvie will have him clean and warm in no time." He started toward the door with Élise. "I believe I smell vin chaud."

Julia checked the time on both of her clocks. The hour was nearly four. She looked toward the wagon and then the barn. "We should probably be on our way." Her clothes would be mostly dry by now. She could change while Luc loaded the animals and hitched the horse to the wagon.

"Oh, madame," Pierre said, opening the door to the house. "It is much too late to leave now. You would not reach Riv until well after dark."

Julia looked at Luc.

He scratched his jaw, his brow furrowed in an uncomfortable expression. "Pierre has invited us to remain here tonight." Luc spoke in a voice that sounded . . . apprehensive.

"We couldn't possibly impose," Julia said, although staying with the Deschamps sounded a far superior option than riding for six more hours tonight. Her backside would appreciate the respite from the hard wagon bench. She wasn't certain what was bothering Luc, but when she tried to catch his gaze, he became busy scraping mud from his boots with a stick.

"I insist," Pierre said. "And Sylvie will insist as well."

"And I insist too," Élise said.

Sylvie came to the door as the others entered. She was holding the baby on her hip. She motioned Julia and Luc inside. "Oh yes, of course you must stay. Monsieur, leave your boots by the door. I will bring dry clothes and towels."

Julia entered and thanked Sylvie for her hospitality. She was delighted for the chance to spend more time with the woman and her family.

Luc removed his boots. He didn't look up when Julia tried again to catch his eye, and she wondered if he thought it was rude to accept the invitation. Or perhaps he worried about Gabi being left alone.

Pierre removed his boots and went directly to the vin chaud on the stove. Apparently, Sylvie had lit the stove to reheat the warm drink. He inhaled deeply, then stirred it and ladled a portion into mugs for himself and Luc.

Sylvie handed Luc a towel. "The barn loft isn't fancy, but it's warm and dry," she said, motioning him toward the washroom.

Luc took the towel, rubbing it over his wet hair. He started toward the washroom without glancing toward Julia.

"And private," Pierre said.

Luc's neck went red.

Julia drew in a sharp breath as she realized with a jolt exactly what was troubling him. She hadn't even considered that the Deschamps would assume that, as a married couple, she and Luc would naturally sleep together.

Her stomach went heavy, her heartbeat grew unbearably loud, and a plunge into the Arctic Sea wouldn't have been able to cool the blush that spread like wildfire over her skin. Julia was beyond embarrassed. And also ashamed. *This is what comes of telling untruths*, she scolded herself. But the thing that affected her the very deepest was Luc's reaction. His utter mortification at the implication that the two of them wished to be alone together was the most humiliating thing of all.

Julia's mind buzzed, and when she glanced up, she saw the Deschamps were all watching her. It took a moment of recollection before she realized Sylvie had spoken to her.

"Are you well?" Sylvie asked again. "Please do not feel uneasy about being our guest. It is no imposition at all."

"I am perfectly well." Julia blinked herself from her anxious thoughts and forced a smile, flustered by what would be perceived as a rude reaction to her hosts' invitation. "I am delighted to remain here." She smiled wider. "And now, Élise, you will have the chance to finish your drawing." She glanced at the washroom door. "And if you ask him, Luc might draw a picture as well. He is an artist like you."

Élise looked toward the washroom and grinned, joining her father on the sofa and showing him her latest work of art.

"How may I help you, Sylvie? Should I set the table for supper?" Julia knew from experience that keeping her hands busy would push away her anxious thoughts. She glanced at the washroom door but forced her gaze and her mind back to her task. She would not allow herself to dwell on the situation any longer.

Sylvie set her to work chopping carrots while she held the baby on her hip and gathered the ingredients for the beef estouffade.

Luc stepped out of the washroom wearing loose trousers that ended well above his ankles, but Julia gave him only a quick glance, feeling the burn in her stomach when she did and not wanting her blush to return.

Sylvie set the baby on her husband's lap. She took Luc's wet clothes and hung them with Julia's, then returned and began to slice the meat.

Pierre handed Luc a warm mug of vin chaud, and at Élise's request, Luc sat on the sofa with the others and examined the girl's drawings.

Julia started chopping tomatoes, and over the simmering sound of the cooking meat, she listened to the conversation on the other side of the room.

Luc complimented the drawings as he turned the pages of the notebook, commenting here and there on specific details—some that Julia had noted and others she hadn't. When he reached the picture of Adeline's cat, he listened to Élise's explanation of why she'd been unable to finish.

"You are an observational artist, mademoiselle," Luc said. "Do you know what that means?"

Élise shook her head.

"You look at something, and then you draw it. Most artists begin this way, having their subject in front of them as they work. And I can see you've practiced it. But the next step is to draw something from memory."

"I don't think I can do it," Élise said. Her voice sounded discouraged. "I don't remember well enough."

Julia glanced across the room. Pierre had moved the baby to sit between his legs on the floor and was helping him stack blocks. Or, from the look of it, Pierre was stacking blocks in front of the baby, and Adrien was trying to fit them into his mouth.

Élise sat with her notebook on her lap, and Luc held her pencil box.

"Drawing from memory is difficult," Luc said. "And it requires practice. First of all, you must look at things differently. All the things around you. Look at them closely, as if you were going to draw them, even if you aren't. Memorize details that you might forget. You won't be able to do it all at once. But with practice, you will become better at looking. And then better at remembering."

He took a pencil from the case. "May I demonstrate in your picture notebook?"

She nodded.

Luc found a blank page, and Julia could hear the sound of his pencil scratching on the paper. "My neighbor has a small dog named Hugo. I know the basic shapes of a dog from other dogs I've drawn. Head, legs, ears, body. So that is how I begin." His pencil moved over the page. "But now, I must look into my memory, and I realize this body is too short for Hugo." He used the rubber eraser, then kept drawing. "So I make it longer until it is how I remember. And I think of how Hugo's ears are floppy and the ends are rounded . . ."

A sizzling sound caught Julia's attention.

Sylvie had put the meat into a pan on the stove.

Reminded of her task, Julia resumed slicing the tomatoes. Watching Luc with Élise was unexpectedly tender. *He would make a fine teacher*, she thought. *Or a father.* That thought made her blush again, but this time, the feeling was accompanied by a tinge of sadness. Julia would not be part of Luc's life much longer.

She took the bowl of mushrooms and started slicing them as well.

"Now, when I look at the picture, I think, *What is missing?* This does not quite look like Hugo," Luc said. "Is Hugo's nose more pointed? His tail longer? And sometimes I don't remember. And often my picture does not look exactly like the subject in my mind. But that is where the practice comes in."

"You must practice *looking*," Élise said thoughtfully. "And *remembering*."

Luc nodded. He turned back to the picture of the goat. "Now, if you'd like, you can practice with this goat."

"Guignol," Élise said.

Luc's brow rose, and his lips twitched at hearing the name. "Leave your notebook inside and let us go observe Guignol. Study him thoughtfully, look at details, then come back inside and draw what you remember. Perhaps, Pierre, you will join us?"

"Eh, oui." Élise's father nodded. He stood and lifted the baby high into the air and then lowered him, smiling at Adrien's laugh. "I imagine le garçon, he would enjoy the goats as well." His daughter took his hand, and they followed Luc outside.

"I never love my Pierre as much as when I see him with the little ones," Sylvie said when the men and children had left. "You must feel the same, non?"

"Oui," Julia said before she realized what she was agreeing to. She pulled her gaze away from the window overlooking the rear garden and smiled, but the sad feeling returned and, with it, an ache.

Julia set the table while Sylvie made the estouffade sauce and baked the bread. Luckily, Sylvie chatted about cooking and children and the trip they would take to the winery in Cavaillon when the grapes were ripe instead of asking more intimate questions.

By the time dinner was finished, Luc and Élise had gone out to see the goats three times. Each time, they returned and Élise set to work. She furrowed her brows, her face serious as she added to the picture. The pair would discuss the details she was uncertain about, then go back to look. Pierre and Adrien would accompany them, but Julia noticed after the second time, it was Luc's hand Élise held as they walked down the path to the paddock.

"Come, it is time to eat," Sylvie announced, holding up a hand to stop her daughter's protest before it began. "Élise, you may show us your picture once dinner is finished."

The six sat at the table. Sylvie tied Adrien into a high-backed chair with a dishtowel to keep him from falling over and sat beside him, cutting soft carrots into small pieces with her fork and putting them on the table where he could grasp them. Everything else was kept well out of the baby's reach.

Pierre sat at the head of the small table, motioning for Luc and Julia to take the chairs on either side of him. Julia sat beside Adrien, and Élise sat across from the baby, next to Luc.

Pierre offered a prayer, and they tucked in to the meal.

The food was delicious and simple, made better by the happy surroundings and loving family.

Pierre described in detail the wagon-removal procedure, and Luc smiled at the appropriate times during the story, adding a detail here and there. But Julia could see he was still bothered. His gaze met hers a few times, but he continued to look uncomfortable.

Élise talked at length about her pictures and the goats, and as the conversation surrounded Julia, her thoughts could not be pulled from the loft in the barn and, more specifically, Luc's unease at the situation.

"You seem tired," Sylvie said once the meal was finished and she and Julia were cleaning the dishes. The men and children had returned to the blocks and artist's notebook.

"All the travel, I suppose," Julia said, hoping her hostess didn't think her rude. She needed to shake her gloom and be polite company.

"Eh, oui." Sylvie nodded. "And you have another day of it ahead. You will want to go to sleep early."

Julia couldn't bring herself to answer.

Élise revealed her goat drawing once the women joined them in the sitting area. Her parents clapped and praised the artist, making the young girl's face glow with pride. Julia complimented her as well, pointing out specific details she could tell Élise had given particular care to.

Pierre and Luc chatted about vines and olives, and Sylvie fed the baby.

Élise's eyes grew tired, and she laid down her head on her father's lap.

Luc took her notebook, holding it on his lap. He sketched as he and Pierre talked.

Julia joined in on the conversation a few times but for the most part was content to listen.

After a while, Sylvie put the baby and Élise to bed. She brought blankets and pillows for Julia and Luc.

Pierre brought a lantern. "Moon's bright, but the loft, it will be dark," he explained.

Julia yawned.

"Thank you again for your hospitality," Luc said. He put away the pencil and gave the notebook to Sylvie.

She glanced at the page he'd been sketching on, then looked again and gasped, pressing her palm to her chest. "Oh, *mes bébés*." She turned the book around, showing a realistic sketch of Élise and Adrien. The children were beautiful.

"It is splendid," Pierre said. He patted Luc on the shoulder. "The perfect gift. Merci, Luc."

"They are such angels." Sylvie took the scissors from her mending basket and carefully slit the page, removing it from the notebook. She set the picture carefully on the mantel and stepped back, clasping her hands. "I shall find a frame for it. This drawing, it is such a treasure when babies grow so quickly. I cannot thank you enough."

Luc looked self-conscious at the praise. "You're welcome."

"*We* can't thank *you* enough," Julia said. "I don't know what we would have done . . ."

"Think nothing of it." Sylvie swatted her hand through the air in a motion that reminded Julia of Gabi. "Now, the two of you sleep well, and we will see you for breakfast."

Julia glanced at Luc. He was gathering the pillows and blankets.

She picked up the lantern, and the two bid the Deschamps good night and walked into the cool night, following the path toward the barn.

CHAPTER FOURTEEN

LUC TUCKED THE PILLOWS AND blankets under his arms, freeing his hands to push open one of the large barn doors. He stepped aside, motioning with a tip of his head for Julia to enter.

The inside of the building was dark. Julia held up the lantern and stepped inside, illuminating a vast, open space. She could smell the horses but couldn't see the animals in the shadows.

"Pierre told me they plan to establish their own winery one day," Luc said. His voice echoed off the rock floors and high ceiling.

"I hope they do." Julia glanced upward, as if she might see the loft.

"Until then, they've an enormous empty barn for just one horse. This way." Luc started toward the far end of the building. "Above the horse stalls." They crossed the room. The Deschamps' horse and Luc's nickered in the shadows as they neared. They came to a ladder near the wall, and Luc motioned upward with his chin. "Up there."

Julia nodded. She raised the lantern, trying to see what was at the top of the ladder, but above her was only darkness. She put a hand on a ladder rung, and then a foot. But she stepped back, hesitating. She wasn't certain she could climb up while she was holding the lantern, not if she was to keep the long skirt out of the way. And what would she find when she reached the top? "Will you go first, Luc?"

He bundled the blankets and pillows into one arm and climbed up quickly using the other hand. He left the bedding, and then he returned part of the way back down, holding out his hand for the lantern.

Julia gave it to him, and he held it above her so she could see as she climbed. The wood of the rungs was rough, and her boots slipped a few times. She climbed slowly, making certain to step carefully and not to catch the skirts under her boots. When she reached the top, Luc took her hand, and she stepped onto the floor of the loft.

"Watch your head," Luc said.

Julia ducked down, noticing the thick beams that ran along the ceiling. She imagined it would be quite easy to smack one's head, especially in the darkness.

He led her to the center of the loft, where the sloping roof was higher.

The space was larger than she'd assumed, stretching back to the wall at least fifteen feet. When she took stock of her surroundings, Julia froze. "Oh. I didn't realize . . ." The loft was not a guest room at all. There were no beds, not even a mattress. Piles of hay covered most of the floor, and a pitchfork stuck out of one. "Surely we're not meant to . . ." Her words died when she saw Luc's grimace.

"I apologize, Juliette." He set the lantern down on the floor and removed his hat, looking around the space. The uncomfortable expression returned, pulling his brows together and making his eyes tight. "I didn't intend for . . . I know a fine lady is not used to . . ." He let out a sigh, rubbing his hands over his face. "You have probably never even been in a barn, let alone slept in one."

Julia tried to remember whether or not she'd in fact had reason to go inside such a place. She felt a tinge of disappointment that she could not come up with an instance to prove him wrong. "Have you?"

"Eh, oui. Now and then." He shrugged. "We do not have roadside inns or towns every few miles in Provence."

Perhaps his unease over the situation was not for the reasons she'd assumed. She glanced around for somewhere to sit, but with no options in sight, she remained standing, clasping her hands in front of her. "This seems a particularly nice barn. Though, you're right. I haven't many examples with which to compare it."

Luc looked to the side, and she again suspected the discomfort she'd seen earlier may not be directed at her after all. A bit of her heaviness lifted.

"Is this what's been bothering you?" she asked. "That the amenities here would not meet with my approval?" Seeing his grimace, she knew she'd hit upon it exactly. In spite of the hay-covered floor and the smell of horses, she felt an enormous relief.

"Oui." His voice was low. He folded his arms and shook his head. "I am to blame for all of this. If I'd controlled the wagon . . . And I shouldn't have insisted we misrepresent our relationship. You should not have to sleep in such a place, Juliette." He looked toward the ladder. "If I confess the truth to the Deschamps, ask if you might sleep inside, perhaps on the sofa—"

Julia touched his arm, and his words stopped. "The wagon was not your fault. You let the reins go to catch me. The goats were everywhere, the rain and mud . . . You cannot blame yourself for any of that. Besides, we wouldn't have been in this circumstance in the first place had I not tied poor Fleur to that tree." She leaned her head to the side to catch his gaze. "As for the deception, your reasoning for it was sound." She nodded to hopefully reassure him, then stepped back, looking around the space with a changed attitude.

She was determined not to let him see her apprehension about the sleeping quarters. "Anyway, it is just one night. I am not made of glass, Luc Paquet. This loft is entirely suitable." She picked up a blanket and shook out the folds. "Now . . ." She looked around, trying to decide where to put it. She was not certain of how to go about preparing a bed on the hay piles. Did she just make a nest and curl up inside?

Luc's worries seemed to ease. He tossed his hat onto the hay. He took the blanket from her and held it over his arm while he bunched up one of the piles and then laid the blanket over it, making the hay into a sort of mattress. He handed her a pillow and another of the blankets, keeping the last for himself.

"I'll stay on that side of the loft," he said, pointing toward the shadows near the ladder.

"Merci," Julia said. She sat on the makeshift bed but wasn't ready to sleep yet. Outside of the circle of light made by the lantern, the loft was dark, and talking to Luc kept her mind from wandering into the realm of imaginary fears. She pulled the other blanket around her shoulders and yawned. "I forgot to check on the goats. I hope they are all right sleeping in a new place. I don't want them to be frightened. It is very dark out there. And they aren't familiar with this place."

Luc sat on the floor on the other side of the lantern, stretching out his legs in front of him. "They have each other." His eyes met hers. "And Honey will watch over the little ones. She won't let anything frighten them."

Julia blushed. He had discerned her worries perfectly. She was not only concerned about the goats.

"Pierre and I gave them food and water while we were at the pen with Élise," Luc said.

"Thank you for taking care of them." She looked down, picking up a piece of straw and pulling it apart. "And of me." She spoke the last words quietly, feeling shy, especially in the privacy of their shared space. But she did want him to know she appreciated him. If not for Luc, she didn't know what would have happened to her at the train station in Rivulet. Would she still be there waiting for the train? Or would someone else have come along by now? The idea of a stranger finding her gave her a chill of fear. But hadn't Luc been a stranger when she'd gotten into his wagon? Thinking of him like that felt wrong to her. There were few people she trusted as much as him.

Luc rested on one elbow. His expression was soft as he watched her.

Julia was glad no unease remained between them. She tossed aside the piece of straw and shifted around, pulling her legs to the side and leaning on one hand. The hay squeaked beneath the blanket when she moved. She yawned, but she didn't want Luc to think she was sleepy and leave, so she kept talking.

"The moon is bright, so at least they needn't fear the dark."

Luc squinted for just an instant. "Oh. Oui, the goats. They will be perfectly safe."

She nodded, resting down on her elbow and hugging the pillow with her other arm. It was lumpy and round like an old sofa cushion. "The first night I slept away at finishing school, I was so scared to oversleep and be punished for it that I stayed awake all night. The next day, I was punished anyway, for falling asleep in my etiquette class."

Luc chuckled. "How old were you?"

"Twelve," she said. "Young but not too young to miss supper, apparently."

"Is that why you carry two timepieces?"

Julia considered. She hadn't ever connected that particular incident with her preoccupation with timeliness. "It is likely part of the reason. I do worry about being late. About disappointing people who are counting on me." Her head felt heavy, and her eyes. She slid the pillow beneath her head and laid her cheek down on it. "Sometimes I think that is all I ever do. Disappoint everyone."

"You are too hard on yourself," Luc said. "Too worried about pleasing others."

"It makes me glad to please others," she said. She could hardly keep her eyes open. "Don't you feel that way when you've made a person happy?"

"Of course," Luc said.

"And the opposite when you've let them down?"

Luc didn't answer.

Julia forced open her eyes, fearing what his silence might mean. "You haven't let me down, Luc. I don't know what I would do without you." She nestled down into the pillow, closing her eyes again and pulling the blanket tighter around herself. She could hear that her words were slurred but wanted to make certain she told him what she was thinking. "You've made everything so much better."

Julia didn't remember falling asleep, but she awoke with a shock. She lay in the darkness, heart pounding as she tried to reassure herself that she was safe. After all, Luc was just on the other side of the room. But where was that? She was disoriented, with absolutely no sense of direction, and didn't dare move far lest she fall off the edge of the loft. And could she even be sure that Luc was still here? She listened, hoping to hear his breathing, but instead, she heard a rustling in the hay beneath her pillow.

"Luc!" She bolted upright, panic making her thoughts race. The darkness was suffocating. Was there no window in this barn? "Luc, where are you?" She twisted around, searching for—

"I'm here." Luc's arms went around her.

She grabbed on to him. "Luc, I think I heard a mouse in the hay. What if it climbs on me? It might crawl into my hair. Do mice live in barns?"

"No," he said after a pause. "Cats catch them all."

She sighed, relieved, and felt suddenly weary. "I didn't see any cats," she said.

"They hide. You should sleep," Luc said. "Or you might fall asleep during etiquette class tomorrow."

Julia smiled at his attempt at humor, even though she knew he couldn't see it in the dark. She released her grip on him and lay back down on the pillow. But just as soon as she did, another thought jerked her awake. "What about scorpions?"

"The cats get them too," he said.

"Does Sylvie know to put lavender in the windowsills?" she asked.

"Of course she does." Luc shifted. "There is nothing to worry about." Julia could hear that he was moving away, and her fear came back full force. "Luc?"

"Oui, Juliette?"

Her heartbeat sped up again. "I know this is exceedingly improper . . ." He was still in the darkness.

"Will you hold my hand? Just until I fall back asleep?" She felt silly for even saying it. But the thought of him leaving her alone was more frightening than the embarrassment of asking the question.

"Bien sûr que oui." His voice was gentle.

Julia reached toward him, finding his hand, and her worries immediately calmed. His hand was warm and strong, and she held on, knowing that no matter what dangers might lurk in the darkness, Luc was there; he would keep her safe. And he wouldn't let anything crawl into her hair.

CHAPTER FIFTEEN

JULIA SAT UP ON THE blanket of her hay bed. She'd slept soundly, and the groggy feeling that accompanied a deep sleep lingered. The hay felt warm beneath her, and she let the blanket fall from her shoulders.

"Ah, you are awake at last," Luc said. His head popped up over the edge of the loft.

She rubbed her eyes, squinting as her vision adjusted in the dim light coming from the few windows in the barn. "Good morning, Luc."

He climbed up from the ladder and crossed the loft, already dressed in his own clothes. When he reached her, he knelt on one knee, resting an arm on the other. "Did you sleep well?"

"Oui." She blushed, remembering the way she'd clung to him, panicked, in the middle of the night. "Thank you." Julia blinked and rubbed her eyes again. She stretched her arms above her head and yawned, moving a hand in front of her mouth.

"You've some hay in your hair," Luc said. He slid toward her and pulled out a piece from behind her ear.

"Merc—"

Luc's hand cupped her cheek, and his lips covered hers. He pulled away, standing so quickly that Julia's thoughts scarcely had time to catch up.

Luc kissed me.

Fluttering erupted inside her chest, and she gasped at the intensity. She looked up at him, now fully awake and trying to understand what had happened.

"Excusez-moi, Juliette. I didn't mean . . ."

Julia touched her lips.

"You just looked so . . . I'm sorry. I shouldn't have taken such a liberty." Luc started back toward the ladder.

"Oh." She felt like a simpleton but could not do anything but blink as her mind reeled. *Luc kissed me!*

He turned around and started down the ladder. "Sylvie has breakfast for you in the house. The wagon is ready whenever you are."

Julia sat for a long moment. She wrapped her arms around herself as if to contain the feelings that were trying to burst free. His hand in the night, his arms around her, and now his kiss. Was this how love felt? Everything inside her raced, her pulse was strong and fast, her limbs felt shaky, and her thoughts were scattered. But still she sat, trying to hold on to the feeling. Trying to understand it.

After a moment, she stood, brushing off the borrowed dress and folding the blankets. Her lips were hot, still feeling the aftereffects of Luc's kiss. And she couldn't stop her smile. All in all, it was rather a nice way to wake up.

When Julia entered the house, Élise ran to her. "You are awake at last."

"Good morning, Élise." Julia put the blankets and pillow on the sofa.

"Luc drew our pictures." She pointed to the drawings on the mantel. "Did you see?"

Julia nodded, again admiring the drawings. She could see why Élise and her mother were so pleased with them. They were exquisite.

"Mamá will put them into a frame," Élise said.

"Did you sleep well?" Sylvie came from a bedroom, holding the baby on her hip.

"Oui. The loft was very comfortable. Merci."

"*C'est romantique, non?*"

Luc's kiss came back in a rush of memory, and Julia drew in a breath. "Oui."

Sylvie gave her a knowing smile and a wink.

Élise took Julia's hand and led her to the table, indicating for her to sit. "You have not had breakfast."

Julia ate a simple breakfast of bread and cheese and coffee. She changed back into the clothes she'd borrowed from Gabi, returned the scarf to her hair, and put on her timepieces. When it was time to leave, her eyes burned. She swallowed, feeling unexpectedly sad at having to say goodbye to her new friends.

Sylvie kissed both of her cheeks. "I hope to see you again, Julia, my friend. Perhaps we will one day visit Rivulet."

"I hope you do," Julia said before she realized that if they did, she wouldn't be there. At this thought, her tears broke through.

She wiped them away, kissing Adrien's fat cheeks and embracing Élise.

"Thank you for visiting," Élise said. "And for bringing Honey and Guignol and Spot." She went to the wagon to bid farewell to Luc and the goats.

Sylvie embraced Julia one last time, as did Pierre.

Luc helped her climb up to the wagon bench.

The family watched from their front garden as Luc drove the wagon away.

Julia turned in her seat, waving until they rounded a bend and could no longer see the farmhouse.

Luc handed her a handkerchief. "You are sorry to leave?"

She and Luc hadn't spoken since the kiss, and she was grateful that he wasn't acting strangely. Maybe it had been nothing to him. The thought saddened her further.

She nodded, wiping her eyes, and looked into the back of the wagon, checking that all the goats were still there. "I am very glad the wagon got stuck near this farmhouse instead of another. I've quite enjoyed becoming acquainted with the Deschamps. Sylvie is lovely."

"Pierre as well," he said. "A good man."

"You probably enjoyed having someone to talk to besides Gabi and myself," she said. "A chance to discuss—I don't know—manly things."

Luc smirked at her tease.

"I know Élise appreciated the particular attention you paid her."

"She has determination for one so young. Talent, yes, but the willingness to work to improve; that will take her far."

"You are very patient. And you make a good art teacher."

Luc looked at her for a moment, and Julia got the impression he was evaluating whether or not she was still teasing. "Her parents are so supportive of her art," he said. "I found it admirable, the way they praised her, and also, I admit to being . . . jealous." He spoke carefully, as if unsure whether he should continue.

Julia thought if she said the wrong thing, he was likely to stop altogether. "Why?" She spoke in a gentle voice, hoping not to sound like she was prying but wanting him to know she was interested in his answer and that she would take his words seriously. "Were your parents . . . less supportive of you?"

"My father." Luc sighed and looked back at the road. His gaze was unfocused. "He thought drawing was a waste of time. We had an olive orchard and a large vineyard. He paid five men to help manage the land, run the winery, and harvest the olives and grapes. He worked long hours every day with them. And yet his own son was always to be found off beneath a tree, scribbling silly pictures."

"But he allowed you to attend l'École des Beaux-Arts," she said.

Luc pulled on the reins, directing the horse back to the center of the road. "I pestered him. Begged him. Promised him I would earn back the money he spent on my schooling tenfold with my art. I was insufferable." Luc's lip curled. "Complaining, whining, yelling, accusing him of stealing my dream." He shook his head, breathing out a heavy breath. "The things I said to him, Juliette. What kind of a son . . . ?" He swallowed.

"What of your mother?" she asked, wanting him to continue. Hearing him share something so personal made her heart hurt, but she wanted to hear more. Wanted to understand Luc. Wanted him to trust her with things he spoke of to nobody else.

"Ma mère, she wanted me to be happy, of course," he said. "In the end, it was she who persuaded mon père. She and Gabi."

"They could see your talent," Julia said. "And they knew you had the makings of a remarkable artist."

Luc shrugged. "And yet, that wasn't enough for me. Instructors, the other students, visitors to the school—they offered praise, compliments, and yet I still felt I had something to prove."

"To your father."

"I wanted so badly to impress him. To make him proud," Luc said. "I've thought of it often through the years, wondered why one person's opinion mattered more than all the others. But I have no answer."

"Because he's your father," Julia said. "That is the answer."

Luc nodded. "My parents didn't tell me the blight had killed the vines. I didn't know the farm was losing money while they continued paying for my schooling. Maman was ill, and finally Father sent word. By the time I returned, she had died, and he was too ill to even recognize me."

"Luc, I'm so sorry." Julia's heart ached for him.

"I failed them," he said. "And when I remember how I spoke to him, the things I said . . ." He swallowed hard once more. "I am so ashamed."

"And now you hope to make it up to him, working the farm, taking care of Gabi."

He nodded.

"And giving up your own dreams." She set her hand on his wrist.

Instead of just allowing it to rest there, he put both reins in his other hand and intertwined his fingers with hers, pressing their palms together. "It is what I must do."

Julia rested her head on his shoulder. "I know about trying to impress a father," she said. "When my mother died . . . that is why my father and grand-mère are so protective. They worry that something bad will happen to me." She shifted, leaning more fully against him. "That is why I left the Orient Express to buy the cake. I wanted to show them I could do it by myself. I imagined him meeting me at the Gare de l'Est station in Paris, and when I presented him with the cake and told him I'd navigated the Igney-Avricourt station alone, he'd be so proud. Perhaps he'd realize I am capable of doing things myself."

Luc squeezed her hand.

"But I've proven just the opposite, haven't I?" she said, the familiar feeling of disappointment returning. "I couldn't even do something as simple as purchase a cake without making a mess of things."

"Well, I am glad for it," Luc said. "If not for that cake, we'd never . . ." His voice trailed off, but the unsaid words hung in the air between them as if they'd been spoken aloud.

The conversation stopped, but this silence felt different from the one the day before. Instead of wanting to fill it, to take away the awkwardness, the quiet felt comfortable, like something shared between companions who had exposed something personal and left one another to consider. It was . . . pleasant.

The rain had left everything looking bright and smelling fresh. Occasionally they passed a lavender field or an almond orchard, and the air would fill with the aroma of blossoms. Life moved slower in Provence, and Julia had come to find that she enjoyed the simplicity of home and family and friends instead of the constant worry of schedules and traffic that she navigated in the city. Life here felt somehow fuller of the things that brought happiness—essential things, important things. Even though there were less "things." It gave her a lot to think about.

After a long while, Julia lifted her head. She released Luc's hand and turned around on the bench to check on the goats in the wagon bed. They had apparently become used to the travel. Honey stood, balancing against the movement of the wagon on her hooves, but the babies were both curled up, sleeping beneath her.

"I will be sad to leave Rivulet tomorrow," Julia said, turning back around and giving voice to the heaviness in her heart.

"But you will see your father and grandmother," Luc said. "And l'Exposition Universelle."

Julia contemplated for a moment. She'd looked forward to the World's Fair for so long, reading about the attractions and waiting for the chance to ride the

Grande Roue, to see the attractions and the art. It had occupied nearly every thought for the last months and filled the letters she and her father had written back and forth. But in the days since she'd come to Rivulet, it had hardly crossed her mind at all.

"You must be disappointed to have been kept from the event," Luc said, misinterpreting her silence as unhappiness.

"I am not disappointed," Julia said. "Rivulet has been . . ." She felt heat rise on her cheeks and looked away, watching the mountains in the distance. "I've enjoyed my time here quite a lot."

"Even when you are meant to be surrounded by music and theater and art?"

She bumped him with her elbow, giving a wry smile at his tease. "That was very rude of me to say. I should not have assumed anything about Provence. It has surprised me at every turn."

Luc took her hand again. "Do you return soon to Vienna?"

"The spring holiday lasts for three weeks. I will stay with ma grand-mère on Rue des Barres, then leave Paris two weeks from Saturday," she said. "Classes resume the Monday following."

Luc nodded, and they lapsed back into a silence that was broken only by the noise of the goats and the crunch of the wagon wheels.

Julia wondered if Luc was glad for the quiet. Was he sad that she would leave tomorrow? Or did she read more into his actions than he actually intended? She looked down at their hands, fingers entwined, his wrist resting on his knee, and wondered if the life she was returning to would ever feel the same as it had before.

CHAPTER SIXTEEN

GABI HURRIED OUT OF THE front door the moment the wagon was in sight of the house. She came to the break in the wall and waved, one fist on her hip. The two cats wound around her ankles.

"She was worried," Luc said in a low voice.

Julia let go of his hand. She didn't completely understand the status of her relationship with him, but she felt it was something she wanted to keep private, especially since she worried that her feelings for him were not fully reciprocated. She may be imagining more in his kindness to her than what he'd intended by it.

When the wagon reached Gabi, she clasped her hands. "Oh, mes chères! You are home at last!"

"We had some trouble with the wagon," Luc explained. He climbed down and took Julia's hand to help her from the wagon seat. "Stuck in the mud."

Gabi took his face in her hands, patting his cheek playfully. "You made this old lady worry."

"Luc found us a place to stay for the night," Julia said, "and someone to help to extract the wagon."

"Oh, all this rain." Gabi shook her head, making a tsking sound. "Of course Luc knew just what to do. But still, I worry for *mes enfants*." She kissed Julia's cheeks and pulled her into an embrace. "I am so glad you are safely home."

Julia held Gabi tighter than was perhaps necessary, and longer. But the woman's words had touched her. *Mes enfants—her children.* The reminder that Julia would leave Rivulet tomorrow brought a lump to her throat. She would miss Gabi and her fussing. While Julia loved her grand-mère and knew she was loved in return, the woman wasn't affectionate in the same way. She showed her love through stern correction and constant reminders of the proper way a young lady should act. A warm embrace was something different altogether. And Julia hadn't realized it was something she craved.

A bleat came from the bed of the wagon.

"Oh, you found a goat," Gabi said.

"Not just a goat." Luc smiled at Julia. He let down the back gate and untied Honey's rope. The goat jumped down.

"Oh, she is beautiful." Gabi nodded approvingly.

Luc handed Honey's rope to Julia. He untied Guignol and Spot and lifted them down from the wagon to join their mother.

"Oh." Gabi's eyebrows rose. "And two kids?"

The baby goats jumped around, kicking their hooves into the air, delighted at their freedom after the long wagon ride. Spot leaped onto the low wall.

"Juliette, she did not want to break apart a happy family," Luc explained.

"Ah." Gabi crouched down and scratched Guignol's head. "They are still quite young to be weaned." Her lips twitched. "You have a kind heart, Juliette."

"Do you think Alice will be pleased?"

Spot jumped from the wall, kicking up her feet as she bounced back toward her mother.

Gabi laughed. "How could she not?"

The three ate a meal of hare-and-wine stew before leading Honey and her babies across the yard to the Laurents' house.

Julia fidgeted as they neared the front door, feeling anxious. What if Alice remained angry? What if Honey did not meet with her approval?

Luc's hand brushed hers, just a soft touch that could have been accidental. But she knew it wasn't. Luc understood her worries and hoped to reassure her. She glanced up at him, giving him a grateful smile. If nothing else, she had his support.

Alice came to the door, and Mathieu followed, leaning heavily on his cane in the doorway.

"Bonjour, Madame Laurent," Julia said. She tugged on the rope, bringing the goat closer. "This is Honey."

Alice stepped outside. She squinted as she scrutinized the goat.

"Her milk is sweet," Julia said. "And I hope you don't mind, but we've brought her babies as well."

Luc and Gabi set the kids down, and they immediately started jumping around the garden.

Alice's stern face showed a hint of a smile.

Guignol kicked up his back legs so hard that he fell over. Spot jumped onto him, and when her brother flipped over, she flew off, bouncing away.

Mathieu laughed loudly, bending over and holding his side.

"Guignol and Spot," Julia said, pointing to the goats in turn. "But, of course, you can call them what you wish." She clasped her hands. "Madame, I am so sorry about Fleur. I hope you can forgive me."

Alice looked at her for a moment, and Julia worried that the woman would not ever forget the wrong done to her.

The older woman's face broke into a wide smile. "Of course you are forgiven, Juliette." She clasped Julia's arms right below the shoulders and planted a kiss on each cheek.

Julia blinked. This was the second time she'd been startled by a kiss today. And though this one was not unpleasant, she much preferred the first. She glanced at Luc, giving a surprised smile at the woman's reaction.

The smile and wink he gave in return said he was proud of her. Seeing it warmed her all the way through.

Once they left the Laurents', Luc went to tend to the olives. Julia spent the remainder of the afternoon in the garden with Gabi. The rain had made the soil soft, and the pair worked companionably together, pulling out weeds, separating herbs, and cutting flowers for vases and drying.

Julia told the older woman about the Deschamps family and especially about how considerate Luc had been with Élise.

"Ah, he is so very kindhearted." Gabi shook her head fondly.

"He drew beautiful portraits of the children," Julia said. "Sylvie was so pleased."

Gabi glanced toward the building that served as Luc's art studio. "If that boy could only see what others see in him."

"He could do it," Julia said. "He could display his art, sell it if he chose. He would be known as one of the great artists of our time."

"But he will not," Gabi said. She sighed. "To see a dream die—" Her voice caught, and she cleared her throat. "It is painful, non?"

"Oui," Julia said. She glanced at the building as well, and a thought occurred to her. An idea. She stopped pulling weeds, sitting back on her heels and letting the idea take root as she considered the different complications that might arise and how to manage them.

She was still lost in thought when Luc came into the garden. Seeing him, she smiled and stood, brushing the dirt from her fingers.

"How are the seedlings today?" Gabi asked.

"They appear healthy," he said. "I moved some of the larger pots outside to begin to acclimate them. I'll move them back into the nursery tonight."

Gabi nodded. "The nights are still very cold."

Luc took off his hat and ran his fingers through his hair. "I wondered if perhaps you might like to walk to the lily pond, Juliette."

A thrill shot through her middle, and she smiled, knowing he'd been thinking about her. "I would enjoy that very much."

He nodded. "Is now a good time? Or are you still . . . ?" He motioned to the ground where she had been weeding.

"Of course it is a good time," Gabi said. "Juliette doesn't want to spend her last hours in Riv digging around in the dirt." She stood, setting her trowel in a pot. "If you will wait just a moment, I'll send along a picnic." She started toward the house. "Luc, find that old quilt," she called back over her shoulder. "The one with the yellow roses. I think it is in the chest beneath the stairs."

By the time Julia had washed off her hands, Gabi had a meal packed into a basket, and Luc stood at the kitchen door with a quilt beneath his arm.

Gabi gave him the basket, and he hung it in the crook of his elbow.

"Merci, Gabi," he said, holding open the door for Julia. "We will be back before dark."

"Take as long as you'd like. Enjoy the pond . . . and your time together." Gabi gave the pair of them a meaningful look that made Julia's cheeks heat up, then walked toward them, holding her hands out to the sides as if to shepherd them toward the pond. "Go on now."

They started down the path with olives trees on one side and grape vines on the other. Luc took Julia's hand.

The touch made her palm tingle.

"Wait one moment," Luc said when they neared his studio. He went inside and came back out right away, carrying—along with the picnic supplies—a pad of paper and a pencil box.

Julia took them, wanting to leave one of his hands free so it could hold hers. They continued along, and ahead she saw the end of the rows of grape vines. Beyond was a cluster of trees, and farther along still, hills rose toward the mountains. One was covered with lines of purple lavender, the other with red poppies.

Luc helped Julia climb over the low wall that marked the edge of the property. A pathway ran along the other side, leading into the cluster of trees.

When they drew near, Julia felt as if she had walked straight into a painting. All around, the trees were in bloom with yellow, pink, and white blossoms. Willow branches hung down, speckling the light and shadow beneath as their leaves moved in the breeze. The pond was covered in lily pads with large pink blooms, and a family of ducks swam among them. Stretching over the water was a stone bridge.

Julia recognized the place immediately. "From your painting," she said in a whisper. Speaking louder would break the magic of this place.

Luc nodded. He spread the quilt over a flat place beneath the willow.

She sat beside him, pulling her legs to the side and arranging her skirts. "It is . . . this place is breathtaking," she said, keeping her voice soft.

"Oui," Luc said. "Ma mère, she loved it here. She said this is what convinced her to leave Aix and move with my father to Riv. She fell in love with this place as well as with him."

Julia watched the ducklings swimming behind their mother. The air here was fragrant, the sounds were dampened by the trees, and the way the light played over everything was simply bewitching. "I can see why."

Luc turned a page in his sketchbook and began to draw. "Once they married, Father was much too busy caring for the farm to come here often. It saddened her."

"She brought you," Julia said.

He glanced at her, then back at his drawing. "I think that bothered my father. He would rather I spent more time working the land and less daydreaming in my notebook."

"And now you do the work as a sort of penance," she said. "You are punishing yourself."

"I suppose that is partly true." Luc glanced at her again. "But the trees do need tending, whether I enjoy doing it or not."

Julia took a breath. "Luc, I know I've said it before, but your paintings, they are . . . *you* are . . . you both deserve to be recognized among the great artists. I know it. I promise it. You must display your paintings, and l'Exposition Universelle is the perfect place for it."

"Non, Juliette."

"But I don't understand why. This is your dream, Luc, the thing you worked for, that you still work for . . . and yet . . ."

"And yet, I am a farmer."

"But you could be—"

"I could fail once again," Luc said, his voice sharp. "Lose the farm altogether." He clenched his jaw. "A man learns from his mistakes, Juliette. He does not repeat them." He snapped the book shut and tossed it down onto the blanket.

She opened her mouth to argue, but seeing Luc's expression, she stopped. He would not be convinced by words. And she did not want to ruin their last day together by arguing. The idea she'd had earlier came back into her thoughts. Luc didn't believe in himself. Perhaps he just needed someone who did.

"I apologize," she said. "I won't bring it up again."

Luc let out a breath, offering a smile. He looked beneath the towel on the picnic basket. "Gabi packed some bread. Shall we feed the ducks?"

They stepped along the smooth stones of the old bridge until they reached the highest point in the very center. Luc handed her a chunk of bread, and Julia broke off a bit, dropping it into the pond.

One of the ducklings snapped it up. The others gathered, and Julia dropped more bread, making certain to place a larger piece directly in front of the mother duck. One duckling seemed to move faster than the others, and he wove in between his siblings, snatching the bits of bread before the others could get to it. Julia waited until the faster duckling was on one side of the group and dropped a handful of crumbs to the ducklings on the other side. When the fast duckling swam over to that side, she repeated the strategy, making certain they all got some of the bread.

She laughed as one of the ducklings dove down after a sinking crumb, its backside pointing up out of the water, tail wiggling back and forth.

When she looked up at Luc, he was watching her.

Julia blushed. "What is it?"

His eyes were thoughtful. "It is you, Juliette." He took her hand, lifting it and brushing a kiss over her knuckles. His other hand went around her waist, drawing her against him. He held her gaze for just a moment, and then his lips were on hers.

Julia was fully prepared this time. She closed her eyes and let the sensation wash over her. Luc's kiss now was different from the one this morning in the loft. He held her gently, his lips moving softly, as if asking permission. Permission she willingly gave.

She slid her hand up his arm, letting her fingers rest on his neck, and kissed him back. Luc's arms were strong around her, his whiskers scratchy against her cheek, and his kiss deepened. She held him tighter, not wanting the moment to end, not wanting to face the reality that in the morning she would leave Provence, leave him. The thought brought with it an ache that made her gasp.

Luc pulled back, his brows drawn together in concern. "Juliette?"

She shook her head, not trusting herself to speak. She held on to him tightly, pressing her face into the hollow beneath his shoulder. And though she tried to hold it back, a sob slipped out.

Luc held her tightly. He rubbed a hand up and down her back.

"I'm sorry," she said, her voice shaking. "I didn't mean . . ." She pulled back, wiping away her tears. "I am sad to leave Rivulet. Not sad that you kissed me."

Luc raised his brows.

Julia turned back to watch the ducklings, setting her hands on the railing to look over the side, but the ducks were no longer beneath the bridge. "I just wanted you to know—in case you were wondering," she added. Her cheeks burned.

"That is indeed a relief." Luc stood beside her. He laid his hand on hers and gave it a gentle squeeze.

After their quiet picnic, they walked back toward Gabi's slowly, as if hoping their dawdling footsteps would delay the inevitable farewell. The evening was growing dark, but it was still light enough for them to see their way.

When they neared Gabi's garden, Luc stopped. He glanced toward the nursery. "I need to bring the pots inside."

"I should like to see Honey and her babies tonight," Julia said, glad that he would be occupied while she went to speak with Mathieu. In order for her plan to work, she needed his help.

Luc kissed her cheek. He set the quilt and basket beside the garden wall. "I will see you at dinner, then."

Gabi made a delicious meal for Julia's last dinner in Provence: baked ham with herbs and scalloped potatoes accompanied by thick chewy bread and, of course, chèvre. Though Gabi tried to keep up their spirits with gossip and funny stories, the mood was somber.

Julia picked at her food, dropping the occasional bite to the cats.

Luc hardly spoke a word.

When the dishes were cleaned, Julia excused herself, explaining that she needed to rise early the following morning to catch her train.

"I'll drive you to the station at six?" Luc asked.

"No need," Julia said, trying to keep her voice light. "Mathieu has agreed to take me. He has to be at the station anyway." She couldn't look Luc in the eye, knowing his feelings would be hurt. But riding in Mathieu's wagon was essential to her plan.

She went up to the Lavender Room, sitting on the bed and trying to imprint everything about it into her mind. She couldn't remember what other room had felt so much like her own. Certainly not the sleeping quarters in the boarding school that she shared with three other teachers, nor the bedroom in her grand-mère's house, where she was a guest for only a few weeks at a time. But here . . . She smiled, remembering the incident with the scorpion. Here, she felt at home.

The ache returned, but she did not allow herself to weep, not when there was work to do. She watched through the window, seeing the moon rise higher. She would be glad for the light, but it would also expose her should anyone look out the window. She would need to be completely sure that everyone was asleep, and then . . . then she would make certain Luc didn't give up on his dream. And pray for his forgiveness.

CHAPTER SEVENTEEN

ONE WEEK LATER

AT LAST IT WAS JULIA's turn to ride the Grande Roue. Her father had promised her every day since she'd arrived from Paris, and since he, naturally, would not hear of her riding the grand wheel alone, today was the first time he had the opportunity to join her.

Colonel Weston paid the two francs for a first-class car, and he and his daughter climbed inside. An attendant made certain the safety gate was secure, and a moment later, they were lifted into the air.

"One hundred and ten meters," her father told her. "That is how high we are traveling." The ascent took nearly half an hour as the cars beneath were emptied and filled, but Julia didn't mind at all. The sight of the World's Fair from this vantage point was awe-inspiring. She could see the Globe Céleste, where she and her father had viewed a presentation on the constellations the night before. Beyond was the aquarium and, farther on, the Grand Palais and the Petit Palais, both filled with fine art. Between the buildings and displays, moving walkways took visitors to the various exhibits. Above it all, the Eiffel Tower stood proudly, painted magnificently yellow for the occasion.

The Rue des Nations featured pavilions sponsored by various countries, and each had apparently tried to outdo the others. Julia's favorites had been the reproductions of the Chinese Imperial Palace and the enormous Turkish pavilion designed in the Ottoman style with Islamic architecture and beautiful Mosque minarets. She had eaten cuisine from a different land every evening for supper.

When they reached the highest point, she leaned forward. "The view is magnificent, isn't it?"

Her father's hand, unsurprisingly, clamped her shoulder to keep her from falling. "It is, my dear. Well worth the hour-long wait."

She smiled, glad to be with him once again and to have the chance to speak English. Julia had missed her father enormously. He had more gray in his side whiskers than she'd remembered, and the wrinkles that fanned out beside his eyes seemed deeper. Putting together the British artist exhibit had been time-consuming, and it had taken its toll. She sat back, knowing it would set him at ease.

"What shall we do after this?" she asked. "Or must you return soon to the Grand Palais?"

He glanced at his pocket watch, clicking it shut and tucking it back inside his waistcoat. "I've time to visit another exhibit, if you'd like. You've still not seen the magnification of the moon through the world's largest telescope. Fascinating, that. Or we could just enjoy a nice iced lemonade and watch the crowds."

"I would be happy to do either of those things," Julia said. "There is still so much to see. And, of course, we must watch the moving pictures again. If not today, then . . ." Her voice trailed off as a person below caught her attention: a man in a bouclé coat and a wide-brimmed farmer's hat. She leaned forward again and felt her father's hand clamp her shoulder. Could it be him?

"Luc!" she yelled.

"My dear, really." Her father shook his head as he glanced at the other people in the car. "Most unbecoming of a young lady to holler like that. What would your grandmother say?"

Julia pointed downward. "But, Father. It is *him*. Luc Paquet." She was sure of it. "Luc!" she yelled his name again, waving her handkerchief over her head.

This time, he turned, looking up. Even from this height, she could see the moment he recognized her. He lifted his hand.

He is here. Julia gripped the bar of the safety gate as her heart pounded uncontrollably. He had come after her.

Her father held on to his hat, peering down over the Grande Roue car. "Luc Paquet, the artist from Provence?"

"Yes." Julia was breathless with anticipation. "The same." The Grande Roue moved impossibly slowly in its descent, and by the time her car reached the bottom and the attendant opened the gate, she practically jumped out of her seat.

She opened her parasol, and once her father had climbed out of the car, she took his arm, pulling him forward.

Luc waited at the exit. He stood stiffly and watched her with an unreadable expression.

Julia couldn't erase her smile. As she drew nearer, the familiar fluttering started in her chest. "Luc, I am so happy to see you." She was pleased at her choice of clothing this morning. She wore a white gown with lace embellishments that flattered her figure splendidly, and on her hat were colorful silk flowers and ribbons. She motioned between the two men. "Please allow me to introduce my father, Colonel James Weston. And Father, this is Luc Paquet."

"Bonjour, Colonel Paquet." Luc inclined his head. His expression did not change.

Her father tipped his hat. "Glad to meet you at last, sir. I must thank you for the care you gave my daughter." He spoke French slowly, with a heavy accent. "Always finding trouble, this one." Colonel Weston chuckled, patting Julia's hand where it rested on his arm. "The wrong train. How does one manage that?"

"I—" Luc began, glancing at Julia as if wondering if he was meant to give an answer.

"But that's all in the past," her father continued. "My daughter is safe, thanks to you, monsieur—and she found quite a prize in Provence. An unknown artist of your talents was an extraordinary discovery. The entire art community is talking about it."

Luc looked at Julia. His expression wasn't pleased.

"Have you seen your painting in the Grand Palais, Luc?" she asked.

"I have not. Not yet."

Julia felt another thrill. He had come to find her before even seeing the artwork.

"I believe you'll be very pleased, Monsieur Paquet," Colonel Weston said. "Julia found a splendid frame, and my French colleague has placed it beautifully among the other impressionists from your country, though I believe yours has drawn the most attention."

Luc cleared his throat, apparently uncomfortable with the conversation. "Sir, with your permission, I hoped to speak with Miss Weston alone for a moment."

"Of course." Colonel Weston smiled. He patted Julia's hand again and then gently took it from his arm, squeezing her fingers affectionately. "I should return to the Grand Palais anyway. Why don't I meet you there. I would be pleased to introduce you around, show you some of the highlights. Shall we say in two hours? It will give Julia a chance to show you some of the exhibits."

"Merci, monsieur," Luc said, inclining his head again.

Colonel Weston tipped his hat and strode away.

Julia took Luc's arm, and they started toward the river. People passed, wearing costumes from every imaginable nation. Music sounded from different quarters, some songs familiar, others exotic. The trees overhead were in blossom, the air was warm, and she felt utterly happy. She directed him toward the Pont Alexandre III, the bridge that would take them to the Rive Droit and the Grand Palais.

Julia spoke first. "I can't believe you found me, Luc. There are so many people here."

As if to prove her point, the crowd pushed them to the side of the road as an Egyptian caravan walked past. Julia stared at the camels with their flat feet and rounded humps and apologized as she bumped into a woman wearing an extremely fancy peach-colored hat.

Luc led her out of the crowd. "I went from the train station to your grand-mère's house on Rue des Barres. She directed me to the Grande Roue." His voice sounded distracted. Hardly surprising with such surroundings. A group of Chinese women strolled past wearing silken gowns and teetering on miniature feet.

"Well, it was very fortunate you came just when you did; otherwise—"

Luc stopped. He took Julia by the arm and led her to the rail overlooking the Seine and turned, placing her back against the rail and facing her directly. "Juliette, how could you do this?" His voice was low and sharp, and there was no mistaking the anger in his eyes.

She blinked, holding tightly to her parasol handle. "How could I . . . ?"

"You took my painting after I specifically told you I did not want it displayed." He pressed his fingers to his forehead. "What on earth made you think you could do something so . . . despicable?" Luc clenched his jaw. His lips pressed together, and he breathed through his nose in heavy puffs.

Julia was shocked. She'd thought Luc would be initially upset but, after he'd gotten used to the idea, he would secretly be pleased. She was certain this was what he wanted—even if he didn't yet realize it.

"You must see it, hanging with the others," she said, forcing a cheerful tone. Once he calmed, he would see—surely he would. She just had to convince him. "It has been very well received. My father has had many inquiries about you and about your work. He's beside himself because I made him promise to respect your privacy, but . . ."

Her voice trailed off when she saw he was shaking his head. His frown had only grown deeper, his face redder, his jaw tighter.

"Juliette, you betrayed my trust." His voice had lowered, and in it she could hear hurt along with the anger. "You—how could you?" He clenched his fists.

"Luc." Julia touched his arm, but he pulled away. She winced but pressed on. "I know it was a rather drastic measure, but I—"

"You crept into my studio in the middle of the night and stole something precious to me—a secret I entrusted you with. I can only assume you had Mathieu's help to hide it and bring it to the train station. And now it is hanging . . ." He motioned with a wave in the direction of the Grand Palais. "I would not have ever believed you capable of such a deception."

"Luc—"

"And for what?" He spoke over her, his voice growing louder. "To prove to your father that you could do something right after all?"

His words hurt. "Of course not." Her voice shook, and she swallowed hard. "I did it for you."

Luc crossed his arms. He shook his head, and his eyes were tight. "You cannot fix everything, Julia. You do not always know what is best. You cannot just know someone for five days and think it is your duty to steer their life on the course you deem to be right."

"That isn't—"

"I cannot forgive you for this." He clasped his hands behind his back and motioned to the side with a jerk of his head. "Now, come along. I'll deliver you home."

Of course he did not think she could walk alone. He was no different from her father and grand-mère and Frau Maven and all of them. "I am perfectly capable of finding my own way." She turned and started away with quick footsteps, not wanting him to see the tears that trailed down her cheeks. But after only a few steps, she spun and came back, knowing if she did not give voice to her feelings now, she would not have another chance.

She stood directly in front of him and wiped her eyes with her gloved fingers. "Luc, I am sorry that I hurt you. But I did not do it . . ." She shook her head, frustrated that she couldn't find the words. Her tears were flowing full force now, and she sniffed. "I needed you to know that I believe in you, even though you do not believe in yourself." She wiped her eyes again. "I see greatness in you, and I wanted more than anything for you to know that you are not a failure."

Luc stood motionless, watching her.

"And I also . . . I wanted a reason to return to Riv." She wiped at her nose. Her cheeks were burning, and she knew she was making a scene. "To bring back the painting and have a chance to see Gabi and the goats and the Lavender Room again . . ." She looked down, unable to meet his eyes. "But most of all, I wanted an excuse to see you." The words were practically a whisper.

Julia didn't raise her gaze to his. She didn't reach for his hand, didn't try once more to convince him that what she had done was in his best interest. She was exhausted, and her heart ached. She'd confessed her feelings, explained herself, but knew there were no more words to say.

So she fled into the crowd.

Luc did not call after her or attempt to stop her, and she did not turn back. She rushed across the bridge, through the exhibits, and beneath the Eiffel Tower. A young woman in her path bumped into a man, making him spill a lemonade ice onto her dress. Julia veered around them without stopping, exiting the World Exposition through the elaborately arched entrance, and continued on until she found a quiet bench in a park.

She fell, breathing heavily, onto the bench, not caring that her white dress would likely show dirt marks. As her parasol fell to the ground, sobs erupted, and she felt like they were being pulled out of her chest. Her eyes hurt, and her shoulders shook. *This must be what it is to feel one's heart break.* The pain was almost more than she could bear.

And all of it was her fault.

She'd ruined everything—again. But this time, it was so much worse. She hadn't been trying to prove her competence to her father or to please a teacher. She'd done this all for Luc, but he hadn't understood.

And now he was lost to her.

CHAPTER EIGHTEEN

JULIA STARED OUT THE WINDOW of the Orient Express. The night was dark, and she saw nothing but the occasional cluster of lights when they passed by a village or a town. She didn't wear either of her timepieces, not really caring about which stops the train made or when they would arrive. Her father would tell her.

An attendant passed through the lounge car, offering to refill her tea, but she declined. Hers had already gone cold, but she didn't care about that either.

Her thoughts traveled back to this same train and the journey she'd taken three weeks earlier. It seemed a lifetime ago. Julia was a different person now from the girl who'd snuck out of her sleeping compartment to buy a cake. She was also a different person from the girl who'd arrived at Gare de l'Est five days later carrying only an evening gown, a wrap, a handbag, and a painting covered in a lavender sheet.

She felt tired and sad and . . . empty. Her heart still ached when memories of Provence and Luc entered her mind. So she worked to keep them out. She'd found if she just stared, she could spend hours this way, with no thoughts at all.

Colonel Weston took the seat on the other side of the table. He still had on the formal suit he'd worn to dinner. Julia hadn't changed either, but she hadn't put on the gown she'd worn last time she'd ridden the Orient Express, though it was by far the finer dress. It was another memory. "We are nearing the Igney-Avricourt station," he said. "Fancy a cake?"

Julia could hear in his voice that he was worried about her, but she shook her head as the memory of that station three weeks earlier punched through her carefully created nothingness with a jolt of pain. "No, thank you." She put on a happy smile but knew that it looked forced.

"My dear—"

"I am all right, Father. Just tired," she said for the thousandth time. Seeing that he was not going to be content with that explanation, she turned toward him and made herself engage. "Dinner was very good, wasn't it?"

"It certainly was. Don't know if I've ever had such tender veal. And the sauce on the potatoes . . ." He made a smacking sound. "Delicious."

"So delicious," she said, trying to imitate his enthusiasm. She'd hardly tasted her meal, and if he had asked what was served, she would not have been able to tell him.

Her father indicated another table, the one he'd been at until joining her a few moments earlier. "Nice chaps, those," he said.

She glanced at the group of men. They were all older—close to her father's age—and Julia imagined Colonel Weston had been telling them about the Twilight Tour, an art tour of Europe led by one of his friends, Professor Haskins.

Her father leaned back in his chair. "Quite enjoyed playing cards with them."

A thought struck Julia. "Do you know a man named Nicholas, Father?" she asked, not letting herself think of the other memories associated with the man. "I met him on my way to Paris. He seemed familiar, but I could not quite remember from whence I might recognize him. I thought perhaps he was an acquaintance of yours."

Her father frowned. "Nicholas? Has he a surname?"

"I don't know it. He introduced himself as just that."

Colonel Weston shook his head. "I can think of only one Nicholas. Strange chap, might have been Prussian or perhaps Hungarian. Wore all black. Rather eccentric, I'd say. Met him years ago. On this line, actually. The Orient Express was still a few years from completion." He leaned back in his seat, his eyes looking distant. "Introduced me to your mother." The last words were spoken softly.

"You met mother on a train?"

He nodded. "Formally, yes. A rather funny story, actually."

"You've never told it to me."

His smile was sad. "I apologize, my dear. Sometimes memories . . ." He let out a sigh. "The pain never fully leaves, does it?"

Julia shook her head, feeling tears very near the surface.

"Claire was traveling home from Vienna with your grand-mère, and I from fighting the Ashantis in Africa." He looked back at the darkened window. "I switched trains at the Igney-Avricourt station, and after living on military rations, Frau Spreitzer's gugelhupf cake smelled too delicious to pass up. I purchased my cake and found a bench where I could eat it."

Julia leaned forward.

"A young woman sat on the other end of the bench. She was so beautiful." He sighed again. "I offered her some cake, apologizing that I had no fork or knife, and fully believed she would decline. She looked extremely proper, you see, hands folded politely . . . I still remember the blue gown she wore. Little flowers on the shoulders and a lacey bit here." He motioned to his neck.

"Did she eat the cake?" Julia asked. The story enthralled her. Her father had rarely spoken of her mother before, and never in such a romantic manner.

"She certainly did." He grinned. "Pulled off a white glove and broke off a piece with her fingers, then popped it straight into her mouth."

"Oh my." Julia opened her eyes wide. "Grand-mère must have been outraged."

"Your grand-mère had encountered some former acquaintances at the station and was chatting with them. She didn't even notice, fortunately for me. That woman frightened me more than all the warriors in the Ashanti nation."

Julia laughed, trying to picture her father, young and handsome in his red-coated uniform offering cake to a refined young woman.

Colonel Weston's smile softened again. "Claire did have such a mischievous streak." He stared out the window for a moment before blinking and looking back at Julia. "But it is Nicholas you asked me about. Claire and I parted after our brief meeting, and I boarded the train, thinking I'd never see that lovely young woman again. I'd just entered the dining car when the man approached and introduced me to Claire and her mother. Imagine our surprise at being on the same train." He looked at Julia, his eyes squinting. "The funniest thing . . . I remember he had an old-fashioned-looking pipe, and I could have sworn the tobacco smelled just like the gugelhupf cake. Funny how memories become muddled over time, isn't it?"

"What happened then?" Julia asked.

"We took dinner together, the four of us. Then Claire and I corresponded by mail for a few months, and then . . ."

"Then you married."

"And a year later, she gave me the most wonderful gift." Her father put his hand over hers. His eyes were wet. "I'd never have endured her loss if I didn't have you, my dear."

Julia squeezed his hand. Her father, a military man, rarely showed any kind of emotion. She held on to the moment, treasuring it.

The train whistled, then slowed, and the conductor announced the Igney-Avricourt station.

Her father cleared his throat and stood, taking a handkerchief from his pocket and wiping his nose. "Yes, well. I believe I'll go for some cake."

"Do you want company?" Julia asked.

He cleared his throat again. "Not necessary, my dear. I'll return promptly."

Julia let him go, thinking he perhaps wanted to be alone with his memories. And wishing she wasn't alone with hers.

She thought of his story and the softness in his eyes. She'd never considered her parents' relationship to have been romantic. Never thought of them as young people laughing and falling in love. Hearing it brought a bittersweet sorrow that blended right in to her melancholy. She stared through the window, seeing steam and gas lamps and nameless people moving through the gloom.

Colonel Weston returned just as the train left the station. His cheeks were flushed, and his hands were surprisingly empty.

"Where is the cake?" she asked.

"Oh." He glanced toward the door and scratched his cheek. "I—there was no cake today."

"Frau Spreitzer had no cake?"

He shrugged, glancing at the door again and wiping his forehead with a handkerchief. "Can you believe it?"

"Father, are you feeling all right?"

"Yes, yes, of course." He cleared his throat and sat, drumming his fingers on the table. "Time to turn in for the night, don't you think? Goodness, I certainly am tired." He yawned dramatically.

Julia stared, not knowing what had come over her father. Perhaps his strange behavior was an aftereffect of his earlier emotion. Or maybe, having found no cake, he'd sought out a liquor vendor instead. Either way, he was right. They could both use a good night's sleep.

Julia rose and stood beside the table, waiting for him to accompany her to their compartments in the next car.

But he didn't stand, just fidgeted with his fingers.

"Are you coming, Father?"

"What? Oh yes. You go ahead, dear. I'll be along presently."

"But you said—"

"Think I'll have one more cup of tea. But you mustn't wait on my account. Run along; that's a good girl."

Julia studied his face for a moment, but her father wouldn't meet her eye. He caught the attention of an attendant, motioning the man toward him.

Apparently, he wished to be alone. "Good night, Father."

"Good night, my dear." His eyes darted to the door.

Still wondering what could have possibly come over her father, Julia left the dining car and stepped into the first-class carriage.

The conductor greeted her with a tip of his hat. "Your compartment is ready, Mademoiselle Weston." He watched her closely, with a strange expression.

"Thank you." Julia turned away, wondering what exactly had gotten into everyone. She unlocked her compartment door and stepped inside, removing her hat. And froze, hands on her hair. Her first thought was her compartment had not been prepared for the night. But that concern was only fleeting. She stared at the bench beneath the compartment window.

Three paintings were there, propped up on the seat. And she recognized the artist immediately. Her heart squeezed. She dropped her hat and the hatpin on the bench, moving closer to the canvases.

The pictures were painted in pastel colors, using impressionist style, making them appear as a fleeting wisp of memory. Her breath caught. Each contained the same subject—Julia herself. She studied the first. She was sitting on a bench outside the Rivulet train station in an evening gown with wilted feathers in her hair. Her gaze was cast downward, and she looked completely miserable.

In the second painting, Julia wore peasant's clothing. She walked in the rain along a gravel path, leaning forward and pulling a rope that led a trio of goats. A chuckle escaped at the memory, sounding loud in the small compartment.

She moved on to study the last painting. In it, she had just awoken in the hayloft. Locks of her hair had come out of their braid, hanging messily around her face, and bits of straw poked out of it. One hand covered her mouth to stifle a yawn, and the other was raised in the air as she stretched.

A footstep sounded behind her.

Julia didn't turn. She was too afraid to let herself hope.

The footsteps came through the adjoining door from her father's sleeping compartment, and Luc stood beside her, so close she could feel his heat. "I've thought about these moments constantly over the past weeks. These memories. They are . . . they have become precious to me." His voice was quiet, making Julia's heart pound.

He pointed at the first painting, the figure of Julia sitting downcast in the rain. "Here, I felt something I didn't understand. I didn't know then." He pointed to the second. "Here, in this moment, I thought what I felt . . . that it was . . . that I might be in love with you. And here . . ." He pointed to the third, his arm brushing hers as he did. "This is when I knew for certain."

Julia didn't turn. She could feel herself shaking but didn't dare believe this was real. Not after what he'd said at the fair. It couldn't be.

"Juliette." He reached around her to take her hand, turning her to face him. "I owe you an apology. I know nothing will erase the words I spoke in anger. But I do ask your forgiveness."

She kept her gaze turned downward, feeling shy and afraid of letting her heart open, afraid to be hurt again.

He touched beneath her chin softly, lifting her face. "I was wrong. I left you at the fair fully intending to take my painting and leave, but when I saw it in the Grand Palais, surrounded by such glorious works, mine among them . . ." He swallowed. "It was overwhelming. I would never have believed . . ."

"Father said your painting was awarded a prize medal." Julia spoke in a quiet voice, glancing up quickly, then letting her gaze drop again.

"Oui." He tipped his head to the side, catching her gaze. "You were right, Juliette. The Museé d'Orsay, they are going to sponsor an exhibit of my paintings. I have offers beyond what I could have imagined for works that have not even been seen. You knew it, saw that it was possible, and you risked losing our— our friendship to prove it to me."

She smiled, the walls around her heart softening. "I was so worried, Luc. So afraid I would never see you again."

"Will you forgive me?" He took her other hand.

Julia glanced at the paintings and looked back at him. A bubble grew inside her chest, making her feel as though she might laugh and cry all at once. "You remember me at very unflattering moments, Luc."

He smirked, looking relieved that she was teasing. "Juliette, those moments, they mean everything to me." He lifted her hand, placing it on his shoulder, and wrapped an arm around her waist. He tightened his hold, pulling her against him, and kissed her.

Julia lost herself in the kiss, in the feel of him, in the knowledge that he was here, and let the rest of her worries melt away. She kissed him back, wanting him to know how she'd missed him, how she believed in him and always would.

Hearing footsteps, Julia jumped back, her face flaming as her father stepped into the compartment. Luc kept hold of her hand.

A raise of the colonel's brow was the only sign he'd seen anything at all.

Julia and Luc scooted farther toward the compartment door, making room for him to pass in the narrow space.

Colonel Weston sat on the bench facing the paintings. He studied the picture of Julia dragging the goats. "Such a talent . . ."

"Father, you knew Luc was here," Julia said. "That is why you acted so strangely."

He shrugged. "Went out for a cake, came back with"—he motioned toward Luc—"this bloke asking to marry my daughter."

Julia gasped.

Her father looked up at her and then at Luc and shook his head. "Beat you to the punchline, did I, old boy? Sorry about that." His eyes narrowed. "Perhaps if you'd spent more time talking and less—"

"The hour is late," Luc said, interrupting. He rubbed the back of his neck, his face red. "I should take my leave." He glanced at Julia's wrist and then at her neck, where she normally attached the ribbon of her pocket watch, a flash of confusion crossing his features when he didn't see the timepieces. "Juliette, would—ah, might you see me out?"

She followed him into the passageway, closing the door behind her and leaving her father staring at the paintings.

"Luc?" she asked in a soft voice. "What my father said . . ."

He sighed, glancing to where the conductor sat in his chair at the end of the car.

The man stepped discreetly to the side, looking through the window—even though there was nothing to be seen in the darkness—giving them privacy. Luc's eyes pinched as if he were nervous. "I'd prepared a speech, but it seems silly now."

She smiled, feeling sorry for his embarrassment. "Did it involve raising goats and picnics at the lily pond?"

He held up a finger. "No, but I should remember that for next time." The teasing smile dropped away, replaced by an earnestness she'd never seen in his expression before. "Juliette, I know Provence isn't Paris. It does not have all the fine things you are accustomed to. We are simple people with simple lives. Would . . . could you ever be happy there?"

"With you?" Julia slipped her arms around his shoulders.

"With me." Luc put his hands on her waist. He was still, waiting for her answer.

"Luc." Tears filled Julia's eyes, and her heart felt like it would burst. "I would be happy wherever you are. But Provence . . . it has a way of stealing one's heart, doesn't it?"

He smiled, leaning close until his lips just brushed hers. "Just as you've stolen mine."

Photo credit: Jennifer Tolman Photography

ABOUT THE AUTHOR

JENNIFER MOORE LIVES WITH ONE husband and four sons, who produce heaps of laundry and laughter. She earned a BA from the University of Utah in linguistics, which she uses mostly for answering Jeopardy questions. A reader of history and romance, she loves traveling, tall ships, scented candles, and watching cake-decorating videos. When she's not driving carpool, writing, or helping with homework, she'll usually be found playing tennis. Learn more at authorjmoore.com and on Jennifer's social media.

Facebook: Author Jennifer Moore
Instagram: jennythebrave

Enjoy this sneak peek of Heather B. Moore's
Romance on the Orient Express book, coming April 2021:

Until VIENNA

Summer 1900

Ever since Gigi was old enough to know her name, she'd realized life wasn't fair. And she realized that her aunt, Rowena Georgina Ballard, always got her wish. But didn't Gigi's sixty-five-year-old aunt deserve to have her way when she'd seen a thing or two in life, had her own money to spend, and was in fair health?

Except when the wish interfered with Gigi's life. Rowena Georgina Ballard II's life, that was.

Yes, typically, sons were named after their fathers, and daughters might have a middle name after a mother or aunt or grandmother. But an entire name? Warranting a number after it?

Such was the fate of Gigi.

The second.

"Gigi!" her mother hollered from the bottom of the stairs of their London townhome. "Aunt Rowena will be here within the hour, and you've still to practice the sonata she wants to hear you play tonight."

"I'm on my way, Mother," Gigi called.

Gigi hid her sigh because her dear mother had the ears of a basset hound. If there was one thing the Ballard family did not do, it was disrespect the woman who held the purse strings for all of them. Since Father's death two years before, they'd been forced to sell their home, pay off debts, and move into this London town house owned by Aunt Rowena.

"You'd better go," Gigi's sister, Lillian, drawled from across the corridor, where her bedroom door was partly open.

Lillian Rose Ballard had a name not handed down from anyone in the family—a name to call her own.

She was also engaged to be married in three months' time to the esteemed Bart Anderson, who worked at a prestigious bank. This meant that Gigi was officially the least accomplished out of the entire Ballard clan. The age of twenty-four was almost unheard of to be single. A few decades ago, she would have been dubbed a spinster. In the year 1900, she had a little more leeway. But not much.

Lillian's recent engagement hadn't helped curb their mother's apprehension over her oldest daughter's fate.

But Gigi was completely content in her role as a part-time dressmaker. Her mother wouldn't let her work more than a few hours a day since she believed Gigi needed to be well rested for any social events. That included perfecting her piano playing so that her mother could demand a performance anytime they were in mixed company.

With another sigh, Gigi rose from her writing desk, where she'd been stitching piping on a sleeve. She wanted to present her design idea to Mrs. Stanton, the woman who ran the dress shop. Adding unique touches to clothing was something Gigi enjoyed doing; she just had to convince Mrs. Stanton of the value.

Walking into the corridor, she was surprised to see how advanced the day had become. The afternoon sun bathed the front entryway in gold and orange. No wonder her mother was on edge. She hurried down the stairs, then entered the drawing room where the piano sat. Once she settled onto the bench, smoothed out her full skirt, and adjusted her shirtwaist, she placed her hands on the ivory keys.

The notes of the sonata were light, and after a few times through, Gigi felt comfortable enough with it to please her mother. Aunt Rowena was a tad harder to please, and Gigi would not be spared any criticism from that corner.

Gigi was still practicing when the front knocker sounded. She paused as she listened for the butler's shuffling steps. Mr. Carson should have long since retired, but Aunt Rowena was paying his salary, so no one in the town house had a say in his employment.

The knocking sounded a second time before Carson reached the door and opened it.

The familiar murmured voices told Gigi that her aunt had arrived.

After only a handful of moments, Aunt Rowena swept into the drawing room wearing a wide hat topped with artificial flowers and feathers. The plum color of her dress matched the plum-dyed feathers on her hat, and her silver-threaded hair was done up in an elaborate pompadour. Her walking stick completed her bold outfit.

"There you are, Georgina," Aunt Rowena said. "You will not believe what I've come across. We must speak to your mother at once."

Gigi had no chance to reply because her mother appeared at that very moment.

"Rowena, how lovely that you're early."

"Ah, pish." Aunt Rowena waved a gloved hand before she took a seat on a wing-backed chair that had seen better days. "Hester, I've news to share." She opened her handbag and pulled out a brochure.

Gigi leaned forward as Aunt Rowena used some ceremony to open the brochure. She cleared her throat and began to read:

> *"Join Professor Clyde Haskins on the Orient Express for a tour of a lifetime. We will begin at the Exposition Universelle in Paris and spend a delightful day visiting the international art exhibition as special guests of Colonel Weston, the Commissaire Expert des Beaux-Arts. At each major stop along the journey, we will visit world-renowned museums, from the Louvre Museum in Paris all the way to the Hagia Sophia Museum in Constantinople. We will depart from the most important cities after spending a day or two in each splendid location. On the return trip, we will remain on the Orient Express. Once we arrive in Paris, we'll spend another three days exploring the Exposition."*

Gigi's mother looked duly impressed. Gigi, on the other hand, couldn't help but think of all the time and money this type of tour would take. Only the very wealthy could afford it. Someone like Aunt Rowena, to be sure, and those people who drove around in those shiny automobiles. What were they called? The carriage of the future?

"How fascinating," her mother murmured when Aunt Rowena had finished reading the brochure in its entirety, including the amenities on the Orient Express, such as world-renowned chefs and private berths in first class.

Aunt Rowena folded the brochure and, with a triumphant smile, said, "The members of my whist club are all going, save for Agnes, so we need a fourth player. And I have already booked passage. We leave next week."

"We?" her mother echoed.

"I'll need a companion, Hester," Aunt Rowena said. "Although I will be with my two friends, we are all older women. So we will need a younger person with us to fetch and carry our belongings if needed. Bring Lillian in, and we can begin to make plans."

"Lillian?" Mother asked. "She's planning a wedding, and this tour is an entire month long. There is no way that she—"

"Georgina, then." Aunt Rowena's light-blue eyes landed on Gigi.

Gigi straightened in surprise. "Me?"

Aunt Rowena waved a hand. "Yes, you. I don't expect you to appreciate this as much as Lillian would since you're always bent over a piece of lace or sagging hem, but I can't very well travel without a companion. What if there are unscrupulous men on this tour who wish to take advantage of a wealthy widow?"

"Unscrupulous men on an art museum tour?"

Aunt Rowena's wrinkles congregated into a frown. "Are you a parrot? I'll have you know that I'm quite the catch."

Gigi wouldn't laugh, not now. No, that would take place in her bedroom later. But now that she thought about it, there were probably plenty of older gentlemen who wouldn't mind being married to a wealthy woman no matter her personality.

Besides, Gigi wasn't one to judge. She had youth on her side, and she'd had not one offer. Not even Jimmy Dorsal. Everyone had thought he was sweet on her—but then he'd gone ahead and proposed to Mary Wright. It was all very well. Gigi hadn't been truly in love. More hopeful, she decided. That's why she'd been disappointed. If she'd been in love with Jimmy Dorsal, she would have been devastated.

Nearly a year had passed since then, and she could barely remember the wave of his dark hair, the amused gleam in his crystal-blue eyes, the quirk of his mouth when he listened to one of her shop stories, and how when they danced, she felt like the most beautiful woman in the room . . .

And more recently, she'd had three different men pay attention to her, sending flowers, asking her on walks or rides, but then something would happen. Something that Gigi didn't understand. Each one had gone completely silent. First there was Richard Turley, a talented musician. Then there was Phillip Brandon, a banker. Yes, he was ten years older, but they had seemed to be a good match. Until they weren't.

Finally, there was Reggie Mann, who worked with his father at their general store. Gigi had liked him well enough, and she was just beginning to think he might propose when he'd sent a note around, apologizing profusely.

Dear Miss Ballard,

I have enjoyed our acquaintance as of late. I must offer my most sincere apologies because I will have to break our upcoming plans. In addition, I will not be calling upon you again.
    My sincere wishes for your happiness,

Reggie Mann

"You are a catch for any distinguished gentleman," her mother soothed, patting Aunt Rowena's arm. "And Gigi would love to go with you."

Gigi frowned. Was this not her decision? Apparently not, because her mother and aunt had now moved on to discussing what needed to be prepared, purchased, and packed. Two weeks. They were leaving in two weeks.

"What about my job?" Gigi blurted. "I can't leave Mrs. Stanton in a bind."

Both women on the other side of the room stopped talking and looked at her as if she'd just declared that she'd turned into a horse.

Aunt Rowena's mouth twitched. "You cannot be serious, Georgina. This is the trip of a lifetime. Mrs. Stanton can survive among her fripperies and feathers without your help, I daresay. Isn't that right, Hester?"

Gigi's mother's face flushed, but she rushed to assure Aunt Rowena that she was indeed right.

Gigi's heart sank. Aunt Rowena always got her way. Twenty minutes ago, Gigi's life had been predictable and plain, just how she liked it. Now she'd be living in close quarters with her aunt and her aunt's whist club on a train. Well, them and unscrupulous older men.